Journee & Juelz 3

A Dope Hood Love

Written By: Nikki Nicole

Be careful who you love, chasing that hood love!

Acknowledgements

Hey you guys. I'm Authoress Nikki Nicole some of you may know me and some of you don't. I'm introducing myself. This is my eighth book. Journee & Juelz 3 is finally here. Thank you for waiting patiently and continuing to support this release. I really have enjoyed you guys on this journey. It was a pleasure to meet each one of you.

I was in a really good writing space while writing this. Good Lord, Journee Leigh Armstrong and Juelz Thomas have been a pleasure to pen again, but they wore me out. They have their own stance, they've grown a bit.

I want to thank God for giving me this gift to share with you, without him there is no me. I want to thank my supporters, I appreciate each, and every one of you guys. I always say, "If it's something that you want to do in life please do it. Step out on faith you have nothing to lose and everything to gain. I'll support you because you supported me, and I'll help you because you helped me."

It's time for my **S/O Samantha**, **Tatina**, **Asha**, **Shanden (PinkDiva)**, **Padrica**, **Chamyka**, **Darletha**, **Trecie**, **Quack**, **Shemekia**, **Toni**, **Amisha**, **Shonnique**, **Tamika**, **Valentina**, **Troy**, **Pat**, **Crystal**, **Lacresha**, **Latoya**, **Reneshia**, **Charmaine**, **Dominque**, **Ayesha**, **Misty**, **Toy**, **Chanta**, **Jessica**, **Snowie**, **Tay B**, **Jessica**, **Danetta**, **Blany**, **Neek**, **Sommer**, **Cathy**, **Karen**, **Lamaka**, **Bria**, **Kelis**, **Lisa**, **Tina**, **Talisha**, **London**, **Iris**, **Nicole**, **Koi**, **Haze**, **Dacha.** If I named everybody I will be here all day. Put your name here_____ if I missed you. The list goes on S/O to every member in my reading group, I love y'all to the moon and back. These ladies right here are a hot mess, I love them to death. They go so hard about these books it doesn't make any sense. Sometimes, I feel like I should run and hide.

If you're looking for us meet us in Nikki Nicole's Readers Trap on Facebook we are live and indirect all day.

S/O to My Pen Bae's **Ash ley**, **Chyna L**, **Chiquita**, **Misha**, **T. Miles**, I love them to the moon and back head over to Amazon and grab a book by them also.

To my new readers I have two complete series available

Baby I Play for Keeps Series 1-3

For My Savage, I Will Ride or Die Series

He's My Savage, I'm His Ridah

Join my readers group **Nikki Nicole's Readers Trap on Facebook**

Follow me on **Facebook Nikki Taylor**

Follow me on **Twitter WatchNikkiwrite**

Like my Facebook Page **AuthoressNikkiNicole**

Instagram @**WatchNikkiwrite**

email me *authoressnikkinicole@gmail.com*

Join my email contact list for exclusive sneak peaks.
http://eepurl.com/czCbKL

Here's a little something for you guys Journee & Juelz playlist on Apple Music
https://itunes.apple.com/us/playlist/journee-juelz/pl.u-38oWX9bT1oGzaV

Contents

ACKNOWLEDGEMENTS.. 4

CHAPTER 1.. 10

CHAPTER-2.. 19

CHAPTER- 3.. 28

CHAPTER 4.. 34

CHAPTER-5.. 42

CHAPTER 6.. 1

CHAPTER-7.. 9

CHAPTER- 8.. 14

CHAPTER-9.. 22

CHAPTER -10.. 28

CHAPTER-11.. 38

CHAPTER-12.. 44

CHAPTER-13.. 12

CHAPTER-14.. 19

CHAPTER-15.. 28

CHAPTER-16.. 31

CHAPTER-17.. 47

CHAPTER-18.. 49

CHAPTER-19.. 59

CHAPTER-20.. 64

CHAPTER-21.. 67

CHAPTER-22.. 74

CHAPTER-23.. 84

CHAPTER -24... 91

CHAPTER -25.. 98

CHAPTER-26... 102

CHAPTER -27.. 113

CHAPTER-28... 117

CHAPTER-29... 125

CHAPTER-30... 132

CHAPTER-31... 136

CHAPTER-32... 143

Chapter 1

Alexis

Be careful who you love and give your heart too, and who you fall in love with, and who you decide to be in a committed relationship with. I would've never pictured me and Free going through this shit. I knew Free was crazy, but not this crazy. Man, what the fuck, I can't believe this pussy ass nigga. I should've kept my fucking mouth closed. He did all this shit because I hurt his feelings behind his daddy's pussy eating ass. He would never have the last laugh with me. How in the fuck did he think I felt?

I shook my head from side to side not believing everything he just did to me in a matter of minutes. I wiped the tears from eyes with the back of my hand. Free had it all, he had the bitch he wanted. He had a daughter, that I knew nothing about. He had his family, BUT you still wanted to fuck with me why? He apologized but that shit wasn't sincere. His loyalty wasn't with me if it was he wouldn't even have had a child on me.

If I die today bury me a fucking G. Fuck all this crying shit. I'm over it. It's not going to get me anywhere. I'm not going out like that.

I refuse to let this nigga see me shed a tear behind his no-good trifling ass. I'm so fucking pissed Journee got caught up in my shit. She's pregnant for God sake. He yanked her out of the car like a rag doll.

She didn't have anything to do with me and him. I'm over Free I've been with him for years. I wanted to move on just like him.

Alonzo was bae, and I wanted to keep it that way. I don't regret any of the shit I did or said. He doesn't regret his daughter or Giselle. I didn't ask him to choose. He made his choice years ago. I would never put him in this situation where he must choose his daughter over me. I'm not built like that.

"Free if you're going to do all of this shit you might as well kill me, that's only way you need to come. I swear to God you better kill me because if you let me loose. It's murking season."

"Did I ask you to fucking talk? Keep talking that fly ass shit and I'm going to snap your fucking neck. You wanted to play hardball, and let me know about you and my father. The ball is in my court. You're a disrespectful ass bitch. Before I kill you, I want you to remember me. You know I use to be a heartless ass nigga.

You watched me kill countless of niggas. You were the calm to my storm. You've awakened beast that I've tried so hard to keep hidden. I want to take you to Ethiopia and let my tiger lick on you, like my pussy ass daddy did," he laughed.

"If you're so happy with Giselle and your daughter what the fuck do you want with me? Let me live my life and you can live yours."

"It's not that fucking simple, it's rules to the game and you fucked up."

"I fucked up? Free you don't give a fuck about me, stop being selfish. Did you spare my fucking feelings, when you let Juelz know your daughter wasn't his? No, you bragged about that shit. You hurt me, but I accepted that shit and moved on."

"That's the fucking problem, do you actually think I'm about to let you move on and be with another nigga?"

"You don't have a choice you lost me years ago."

"I do have a choice, you don't have a fucking a choice," he argued and gritted his teeth.

He must be crazy, why would I even consider being with you if you pulled this type of stunt. I can't trust you. We can't trust each other it'll never work.

It takes for you to lose a nigga and look back on the situation to realize he's not the one for you. If Free and I really loved each other, we would've walked away first and called it quits, but no we were both selfish. Look where being selfish has gotten the both of us.

Free

Yeah, I'm that nigga, I kidnap bitches I fuck them, spoil them rotten, and take them to Ethiopia and kill them. I love Alexis. I might've not been the best nigga to her, but I loved her.

Anything she wanted she could have. Giselle knew her place. I might have put Giselle and my daughter before Alexis, but she would never step to her because she knew what it was. I had a bitch and she had a nigga. I'm keeping my bitch. I fucked up, but she was going to forgive me whether she liked it or not.

I'm a savage ass nigga and I don't tolerate bullshit or disrespect from anybody. Alexis violated me, so I had to violate her. Y'all might not agree with it, but it is what is. She shot me twice in the chest. She beat Giselle's ass in front of my daughter, and she let my father suck on her pussy. We're even.

I knew all about her running around with Alonzo, yes, I had Giselle too, but I'm a selfish ass nigga. I do selfish ass shit. If I can't have Alexis nobody can. To ensure that nobody can have her. I'm taking her to, Ethiopia so she can learn to accept this shit, and become an obedient bitch like I taught her too.

She can't be with anybody but me. Giselle is on board she knows Alexis is first and she's second. We're all headed to Ethiopia to live happily ever after. I get to have my cake and ice cream too. Journee was just a casualty of war. Kairo wanted Journee she was rightfully his. Juelz fucked up when he came to my house and put his hands-on Giselle, and left her unconscious.

For that reason alone, I had to rough your bitch up too, because you roughed mine up. She's good I didn't bang her up too bad, she's still my sis despite fucking with the enemy. My brother wanted me to secure her right along with Alexis.

Giselle felt some type of way about Alexis coming to Ethiopia to live with us. I was good on Alexis until she moved out of the house we shared and changed her number. I saw her posted up on Northside Drive with Alonzo, and she had a glow to her face. I could tell she was happy, but I was going to rob her of that shit. She didn't even look that happy with me.

What the fuck do I look like, sitting back watching another man make my woman smile. Alexis has life fucked up. I killed my daddy because he crossed me and that's my fucking blood.

Why would I spare her? I love her, and she did that based on me fucking up, but my father knew better, but since he crossed me he's no longer in the land of the living. My mother knew I killed him, but what the fuck was she going to do anyway?

Juelz

Man, this shit is about to finally happen. Eight years later, I prayed to God that he saved her for me. Journee surprised the shit out of nigga today. I couldn't believe she had that shit in her. She had my smile on beam, a nigga was showing all thirty-two. I just knew that I was going to have to kill her after she walked into the party showing off. I couldn't wait to get back to her.

She was tripping that I had to take Mia home, but that wasn't about nothing. I couldn't wait to get back to her and take her home. Mia knew her place and she should've shut the fuck up. I brought her here so it's only right that I take her back home. I was speeding through traffic headed back to Skeets. Nikki was calling my phone, this is the third time that she has called. What the fuck did she want?

"Yeah."

"Juelz where you at?" she asked and cried hysterically.

"Calm down, what's wrong."

"Kairo and Free kidnapped Journee and Alexis," she cried.

"Real shit, are you sure Nikki. Explain this shit to me," I yelled. I had to pullover and hear this shit. I couldn't drive and process this information. What the fuck was I going to tell my daughter, when I picked her up from my auntie's house, and she's going to be looking for her mother?

Nikki ran down the story of what happened. I knew I didn't trust this nigga. I was ready to comb the streets and find her. Nikki said, that Free said he was taking Alexis to Ethiopia to kill her.

I swear to God if Kairo's bitch ass took Journee and my son to Ethiopia. I'm wiping the whole fucking country out. I don't give a fuck if my ancestors came from Africa. It takes 24 hours to get to Ethiopia. I put my life on it I'll get Journee back in 48 hours. I'm one nigga that Kairo doesn't want to fuck with. I'll go to war behind Journee and my seeds that I've sewn.

He just signed his death certificate. It's about to be some slow singing and flower bringing. Ain't nobody fucking safe. In Ethiopia they have real jungles. In Atlanta, we have Zoo's and I'm on my ape shit.

It's about to be a Guerrilla Warfare. Let me call Alonzo and run this shit by him.

My chest tightened up just thinking about if this nigga really took Journee to Ethiopia on some get back shit. Journee is the air I breathe. I should've kept a good eye on this nigga. The only light skin nigga I trust is Skeet. I knew that nigga had a federal indictment out on him.

I looked into him briefly but not extensive like I should've. I should've known something was off with him when I made it back to Journee's and he snatched her clothes off because she smelled like me. He was possessive and a stalker. He was going crazy behind that pussy.

He kidnapped the wrong one, he's going to regret crossing paths and stepping on my toes and taking something that belongs to me, and she's carrying my second child. I must kill him. It ain't no other way. I swear to God Giselle better not have shit to do with any of this. I left her alive for a reason.

Chapter-2

Alonzo

Juelz hit me up with this crazy ass shit about Alexis being kidnapped by her ex Free. I had to look at my phone, this is the craziest shit I've heard. I was riding down by Hollywood about to bust the corner by H.E. Holmes. Twelve had this motherfucker swarmed, and the ambulance too. A nigga was nard for a minute, but today I'm clean as a whistle. I didn't have that pack on me, thank you, Lord.

As I got closer to the scene, and I noticed it was Alexis's truck flipped over. I sped in the gas station, killed the engine, I threw my car into park, and hopped out. I walked over to the scene to see what the fuck happened. I crossed the yellow tape. I didn't give a fuck about crime scene I need to know what the fuck happened here.

Blood, glass, and shell casings were everywhere my heart drooped. An eerie feeling came over me as I looked at this shit. Her phone was up under her truck. The junk she kept in her purse was spilled everywhere.

"Excuse me, sir, this is a crime scene, you can't be here," the officer said.

"This is my fiancé's vehicle, I'm trying to see what happened."

"We're trying to find out also, do you mind speaking with us for a minute over here," the police officer asked.

"Hell no, it's nothing to talk about."

I crossed the street and hopped back in my car. I grabbed my phone out of my pocket to call Juelz.

"Yeah," he answered.

"Look, I just pulled up around there. It's a fucking crime scene. It's blood every fucking where shell casings. Meet me at Skeet's I need to ask Nikki what the fuck did she hear. It looks bad as fuck. There's no way a motherfucka could've survived that shit. I don't understand what was the reason to kidnap somebody the way that shit looks."

"Stay up through there I'm on my way."

"Juelz don't come, man, you'll fucking lose it. If this shit is true we need to focus."

I've only known Shawty for a few weeks, but I was feeling her something serious. She told me all about what she did to that fuck nigga. It wasn't any secrets between us everything was out in the open she knew my story, and I knew hers.

I put it on my mother and she's deceased Free gone see me and I'm going to put his ass six feet deep, just off the strength he violated her, and the crime scene looks horrible. It's about to be a war in the fucking streets rather it's Zoo Atlanta or in the Jungles of Ethiopia.

Nikki

Journee and Alexis thought I was crazy I never liked those two motherfuckas. I never trusted them. I swear to God Juelz and Alonzo better handle their fucking business. It's not a nigga or a bitch out here breathing that can stop me from killing Kairo and Free. My husband can't fucking stop me. I should've shot him in his head instead of pistol whipping him.

How in the fuck am I supposed to explain this shit to my niece, Khadijah, and Khadir? Fuck that, what am I going to tell my mother? This is one conversation that I don't even want to have. I had to say a quick prayer before I made this call. Somebody's going to need it. She answered on the first ring.

"What child, I just left?"

"Where are you?"

"I just walked in the door damn," she sassed and sucked her teeth.

"Kairo and Free kidnapped Journee and Alexis."

"What the fuck did you just say?"

"You heard me."

"Nikki, God is my witness, and he can take me right now. If I make it to Kairo's mother's house and she answers the fucking door. I'm splitting her fucking wig. All I'm going to say is you better FUCKING beat me there.

If I make it there before you, I'm not promising shit. You better call Troy and let her know, I'm about to roll this bitch like some fresh dice at a dice game, and she's going to be singing her ass off at a few funerals. Get Shanden on the phone right now, she better has those obituaries ready. Those Africans just signed their fucking death certificate," she argued.

"Ma. calm down."

"I'm just getting started."

Lord, when my mother is on go it's no turning back. If Kairo's mother knew what I knew she wouldn't even open that fucking door because her life will not be spared. Kairo ain't crazy he wouldn't hurt Journee, but Free I don't know what the fuck to say about him.

I know one thing Alexis better be ok. The words he said to her will be forever etched in my mind until I see her. He was a heartless ass nigga and scorned too. His voice dripped with venom and jealousy it made me sick.

Khadijah

Nikki pulled me to the side. I could tell something was wrong, her eyes were blood-shot red. She had a look on her face that could kill, that could only mean one thing. Something serious had to happen.

"Damn what's wrong with you, why are you looking like that?"

"Free and Kairo kidnapped Journee and Alexis," she argued.

"Kidnapped? You a motherfucking lie, explain this shit to me? Make me understand it."

Nikki gave me the rundown of what she heard, she was on the phone with Alexis when it went down. It makes sense. I started shaking and crying. Journee is pregnant for God sake. I just found out that I was pregnant also. My sister doesn't bother anybody. She has a heart, of gold why would he do that?

"Khadijah now is not the time to cry, you need to boss the fuck up. We need to figure out how we're going to get Journee and Alexis back."

"I hear you but where were Juelz and Alonzo when this shit happened?

"Juelz took Mia home, he's on his way and Alonzo just pulled up."

"Give me a minute, I just need time to process everything."

How was I supposed to explain to my niece that her mother has been kidnapped, and I don't know if she'll be coming back home? To make matters worse, I must be the one to call Khadir and tell him this shit, and all hell is going to break loose.

Journee is my world, I love my sister to death and I refuse to live without her, because of a fuck nigga whose mad because she doesn't want him. He cheated on her. I liked Kairo I never would've thought he was the type of nigga to kidnap a female.

I may be able to help find Journee. I brought her an Apple watch for her birthday it has the find my iPhone app on it. I installed it in case someone ever stole her watch. Let's hope this shit works. I must charge my phone or get to a computer to see if we can get a location.

I would've never thought that Kairo could pull some shit like this off. Why would he do that to her. If Juelz wouldn't have dropped Mia off, then Journee would've never gotten kidnapped. I knew Free was pissed that his dad ate Alexis box but damn you had a whole baby on her.

Khadir

I'm not even supposed to be speaking on none of this shit here. I let Journee and Khadijah do their thing. I like to be heard and felt, but not seen. I'm the youngest in charge and Journee has been my keeper for as long as I can remember. I'm my sister's keeper. She's always looked after me and made sure I was straight.

Journee thought I was in school in Florida, which is partially true, but I'm down here running my father's drug empire in Florida. Khadijah knew what was going on, but I made her promise me that she wouldn't tell Journee.

Khadijah called me crying because Journee has been kidnapped. I looked at my phone I had to make sure that I heard her correctly. She started crying even more. I knew I had a few enemies, that's why I stayed away because I didn't want my sisters to get touched period.

I asked Khadijah did she know who was behind it, and where the fuck was Jueleez?

Khadijah said, Kairo and Free.

"KD, stop crying do I need to come to Atlanta or meet Kairo in Ethiopia let me know?"

"Come here if we're going to Ethiopia we're going together," she cried.

"Stop crying damn I'll see you in a few hours."

Kairo was a real nigga I can vouch for that. He helped raised me, he showed me the game and gave it to me for free. He did some fucked up shit, but I don't give a fuck about none of that shit, what you did to my sister made you my enemy.

I booked a flight immediately to Atlanta because Kairo was about to feel me. If something happened to my sister I would go crazy. He would die a nasty horrible death. Journee told me all about that nigga still being with his wife. He lost any respect that I had for him. Don't ever in your fucking life think it's okay to play my sister. I wanted to kill him when Journee told me that shit. She begged me not too.

I didn't even pack no bags I had everything that I needed in Atlanta. My girl Reagan was coming with me. She's my peace when a storm is coming. I've been kicking it with her for about a year. I haven't introduced her to Journee and Khadijah because they don't think any female is good enough for me, but Reagan is it for a nigga. She was my rider.

Chapter- 3

Valerie

The last thing that any nigga or bitch wanted to do was kidnap any child of mine. I didn't even get in the house good. As soon as the words left my daughters mouth. I was headed back out the door and to Farrah's house.

Yes, I make house calls my motherfucking nickname was Valerie bad ass, that's what they called me out here in these streets. Farrah is the bitch that's going to answer to me today. I should've paid Farrah a visit weeks ago then that slick son of a bitch had the nerve to play a child of mine like she was a fucking fool.

Nigga, you got the game wrong. I breed bosses and queens, and we don't tolerate that shit. I told Nikki she should've killed that slick son of a bitch when she had the chance too. If I was there I would've scalped the fuck out of him with my crowbar. Alexis should've killed Free's ass too. Look what the fucked happened because y'all didn't finish the job.

Those two pussy ass niggas came back and kidnapped they ass. That's okay because I'm going to beat the shit out of his mammy when I catch her. Those two sons of bitches are going to wish they came up out of my pussy when I get finished with them.

I bet you I get some fucking answers today. Khadijah wanted to call me crying. I told her pregnant ass to boss the fuck up, nobody told you to get pregnant because Journee was. She wanted to know how I knew. I might didn't give birth to her, but I know all my kids when something is off with them. She normally drinks like a fish. She didn't drink shit and Smoke kept rubbing her stomach that's how I knew.

You can't run shit by me without me knowing. It's time to put in work now. Get your passport ready we might be going to Ethiopia. I know one fucking thing I better not catch no God damn Ebola bringing Journee's ass back home. I know Khadijah called Simone and told her what was going on, but I ride solo. My Thelma died eight years ago, and I wasn't looking for a replacement. She may not have been here in the flesh, but she was here spirit.

I finally made it to Farrah's house. I parked down the street, popped the trunk. I grabbed my gym bang and walked to her house. I knew I was going to kill this bitch today. I didn't want my car and tags seen. Black was the color I wore.

I had my face wrapped up like a Muslim. I had my gym bag in my hand that consisted of my crowbar and my Mac11. Anytime I make a house call the coroner is for damn sure coming. I'll wait across the street and make sure the bitch is dead in a body bag. I refused to be seen coming through the front.

I went to the back of the house. She had a high fence but the back entrance to her house. It was like a forest in the back. That was perfect. Her kitchen light was on. I knew she was in the house. I watched for a minute from a far.

I had shit to do, so I had to make a move quick. It doesn't take me long to kill a bitch. I put my leather gloves on my hand. I approached her back door and walked in that bitch like I owned the motherfucka. She was washing dishes. I punched her in the back of her head. She turned around and looked at me.

"What do you want with me, if it's money how much?"

"I didn't come to rob you. I came to kill you."

"Valerie is that you?"

"It is."

"What's going on?"

"Those two bastards that you raised, kidnapped my daughter and Alexis. Anytime a motherfucker come at me with some bullshit. I come harder."

"Watch your mouth, those whores deserved everything that's coming to them."

"Oh, so that's how you feel? I always knew you didn't like Journee, but guess what she never liked you either. I'm glad Alexis let your husband eat her pussy. She made that nigga pay like he weighs and your son too." I hit a nerve with that one. She swung at me. I ducked.

"Wrong move bitch."

"Fuck you, I hope both of my sons kill those whores."

I'm too fucking old to be beating around the bush, with a bitch. I didn't come here to argue or go back and forth. I came here to slaughter a bitch. I had my Glock 45 tucked behind my waist. I walked up to that bitch and I started scalping the fuck out of her. I made a fucking mess.

I was satisfied this bitch was lifeless. Don't fuck with me or my blood and think you'll live to tell about it. As I pulled out my Glock and shot that bitch twice in both of her knees. She wasn't talking shit now.

She started crying, tears don't move me. I grabbed my crowbar out of my bag.

I went to work on her, as far as I'm concerned Farrah got everything she deserved. I checked her pulse to make sure she was dead.

I don't need any bitch coming back to life seeking revenge on me. I kept my gloves on. I didn't need anything coming back to me. I cut her gas stove on and doused it with lighter fluid that was on her back porch.

A flame started in her kitchen. I dug a hole in her wall with the crowbar. I found an electrical wire and lit that bitch. No face no case. The whole house was in flames. I left out the same way I came in. I sat in the woods and watched her shit burn to the ground.

Fulton County Fire department and Metro Ambulance finally arrived. I could hear the sirens, that was my cue to clear it. I headed back to my car. I had to witness them carry that bitch out in a body bag before I pulled off. Kidnap another child of mine.

***

The coroner finally came and carried Farrah out. I had the biggest smile on my face.

I had my camera I needed proof to show Nikki and Khadijah how it's supposed to be done. For the record I would never snap pictures with my cellphone camera. I don't need the FEDS geo tagging my shit.

I got in my car and pulled off. I checked my surroundings to make sure nobody was watching me. Kairo and Free have their ducks in a row. Juelz and Alonzo had better bring it. If not Nikki and Khadijah are trained to go. As much as I would like to go to Ethiopia to set it off. I must watch my grandchildren.

Fuck that Skeet might need to call his mother to see if she could watch them. I need to put in work and bring Journee back home. You can put nothing past Africans.

Chapter 4

Journee

What the fuck did I miss? I was yanked out of Alexis's truck and being thrown in the back of a van. My clothes were ripped off me. Why were Alexis and I being kidnapped and ambushed? I knew the smell of his cologne from anywhere. I looked around to see if I saw him.

His scent used to be intoxicating. It's only one nigga that I knew that wore this cologne, Jimmy Choo. His hands weren't covered, and I could see my name tatted on his hand.

He had the brightest yellow skin that I ever laid eyes on. His eyes were lifeless as they pierced through mine. My mouth was still covered with duct tape. We locked eyes with each other, tears seeped through the corner of my eyes.

What did I do to deserve this shit? I loved him, he fucked me over. I'm pregnant and Juelz is the only man I want. I closed my eyes and prayed I made it out of here alive and back to my daughter and Juelz. Lord knows what Kairo has up his sleeve.

I couldn't even look at him I kept my eyes closed. Kairo was a heartless ass nigga if pushed to his limit. I prayed the hardest I ever prayed in my life.

He walked up to me and grabbed my face I refused to look at him. He ripped the duct tape off my mouth and pressed his lips against mine. I kept my mouth closed. I wasn't kissing him.

"Look at me," he yelled.

I refused to open my eyes and look at him.

"You're still hard headed. Put these fucking clothes on. I don't ever want to smell him on you. I hope you didn't think that we were over, this is the just beginning of something new. Just because you're running around with your baby daddy, that shit don't mean anything to me, I will kill him and Jueleez will be fatherless."

I continued to ignore him. I heard the van door open. I opened my eyes a little bit. I saw Free, he walked in and threw Alexis on the floor. Kairo put some different clothes on me. He handcuffed me and Alexis together. He slammed the door. I looked at Alexis.

"I'm sorry," she cried.

"Sorry for what don't cry."

"I got you into this mess."

"Girl, no you didn't, I knew this nigga was coming. I just didn't know he was coming like this. He's been calling me and threatening me through email. He's been by the restaurant watching me. It's over for us and he needs to realize that."

"If things were so simple with me and Free. He's mad that I'm hanging with Alonzo. He handled me like a man.

He made me open my mouth and he stuffed his gun it. I would rather have a dick in my mouth than a piece of steel. Journee I'm not even bothered by him. He fucked me over. He's still pissed about his father," she explained.

"It'll be all right, we have to figure out a way to get out of here. I have this smart watch on my wrist that Khadijah brought me for my birthday. Let's see how smart it is. Take a picture of yourself and send it to Khadijah. Did Free say where we were going?"

"Do you really want to know," she huffed and rolled her eyes.

"Hell yes."

"Ethiopia," she whispered.

"Alexis, you have to be fucking kidding me?"

"I swear Free said that he was going to feed me to his tiger."

"Alexis now is not the time to cry, suck that shit up, we have to make it back home. I refuse to let Jueleez grow up without me and my unborn son. Do what you must do to survive. These two niggas have played us for years, with common whores. It's time to beat them at their own game. My mother always told me to play a nigga how he plays you." The same way I got here is the same way I'm going home.

Alexis took a few pictures and sent them to Khadijah. I don't know how long we'll have service. I sent a voice text to Khadijah to let her know we were headed to Ethiopia, South Africa. Kairo's family had a compound built there and we did also.

I wanted her to tell Jueleez and Juelz that I love them, and I'll see them soon. Kairo got me fucked up, all I ever asked him was to keep it real with me. He couldn't do that, but what I will tell you is that you kidnapped the wrong bitch.

Our house was so beautiful. I loved Ethiopia despite the circumstances I would make the best of the trip.

Kairo was from Ethiopia he knew this city with his eyes closed, but I had some hittas down South in Somalia.

My Queens are trained to go. Kairo used them to help smuggle diamonds. I hired them, and their loyalty lies with me. I'm going to use them to help me kill this motherfucka. He's going to wish he never fucked me over and kidnapped me.

"I don't like that look," she laughed.

I whispered in Alexis' ear what the plan was she was down. Scorned niggas kidnap women and take them to Ethiopia only to die in the end. It's dangerous to want something that you can't have.

I couldn't wait to sneak off to Somalia to link up with Majesty, Eboni, and Pure. The real question is how was I going to get there. I would have to pretend that I was feeling Kairo and we could move past our differences, that's the hard part. Whoever was driving the van started driving fast as hell. Alexis and I held on to the wall window for support. Suddenly, the van came to stop.

Alexis

Journee and I aren't in the best situation, but I have faith that we can make it out of here alive if we stay together. I refuse to be alone with Free without a knife or a gun. Kairo wouldn't kill Journee because he loves her, but I can't say the same for Free. He might kill me to prove a point. I hate that my gun was inside of my arm rest instead of tucked behind my back. I could've shot Free when he picked me up.

The van came to a stop and Free yanked the door open and uncuffed me. He grabbed my hand like we were an actual couple. It's funny Free hasn't been affectionate toward me in years, but as soon as he sees me with another nigga, happy and moving on. He wants to act all crazy, you could've done this years ago. I cheated on Free numerous of times because I knew he was cheating on me.

We're even let it go. I snatched my hand from him and stood in place.

"Alexis, bring your ass on," he yelled.

"Free, why do we have to do this? Go live your life with Giselle and your beautiful daughter. I'm happy for you. The two of y'all deserve each other."

"I deserve you, I had you for ten years and I'm not giving that up over a few mistakes on your part and my part. We can work past it."

"No, we can't I will never forgive you for having a child on me."

"Learn too I'm this close to forgiving you for letting my dad eat your pussy, we'll talk about this shit in Ethiopia." I refused to get on the plane with him. I started walking back toward Journee and Kairo he ran up to me and picked me up and threw me over his shoulders. I started kicking him. He pulled my dress up and dug fingers inside of my pussy.

"Please stop." I tried my best to move his fingers, he was too strong the pilot was watching us. He kept on doing it until we were about to board the plane. He put me down.

I approached the plane and noticed I heard talking. I picked up my pace and was pissed and ready to fight. Giselle, Tyra and Free's daughter was on the plane also. I turned around and Free had a big smile on his face.

"You got me fucked up." I smacked the shit out of him.

If I was broken and upset, I'm over it now. You kidnapped me but your whole fucking family is on the plane, this is a fucking slap in the face. He picked me up and tried to explain.

Chapter-5

Journee

I wanted to spit in Kairo's face. He had the nerve to blow me a kiss. We were on an airway strip about to board a plane. Kairo walked behind me, I could feel him staring a hole in me. Kairo knew not to touch me because

I'm liable to scratch his eyes out after the last encounter we had. I gave him a look that could kill. He picked up his pace behind me. I heard him yelling my name. I started to walk a little faster. The pilot greeted us as we attempted to board the plane. Alexis and Free boarded first, I heard Alexis arguing I ran to see what was going on and Kairo grabbed me.

"Let me go."

"Oh, you can talk now?"

I ignored him I had to see why Alexis was arguing. He was right on my heels.

I couldn't believe this shit what the fuck was this. If they had these skanks, why are we here?

"Let's go Alexis fuck this shit."

"You're going no fucking where," he argued and gritted his teeth.

"Kairo let me go, do you actually think that I want to be here with you and your wife."

"It's not about what the fuck you want. It's about what I want," he argued and snarled his face at me.

"I don't want you, she can have you. Juelz is the only man I want." I walked off and he grabbed me by arm. I jerked my arm and attempted to get out of his grasp.

"Journee, you want me to hurt you? I don't give a fuck how you feel. Get over Juelz before I kill you and his baby," he threatened.

"Do it Kairo and take me out of my fucking misery, it's better than being here with you."

"That's how you feel Journee, what about Jueleez?" he asked.

"Kairo you don't give a fuck about Jueleez don't even mention her fucking name because if you did, you wouldn't have kidnapped me. Leave my daughter up out of this shit."

"Journee," he yelled.

I continued to ignore him. He doesn't seem to get it. I don't want to have anything to do with him. I waisted eight years of my life loving a man that was fucking married.

I called it quits. You didn't even have the decency to tell me that you were married. You laid next to me knowing damn well you were with her. You kidnap me, and this bitch is on the plane too. I swear those two must be some of the dumbest females.

Y'all are willing to be here and y'all are cool with this shit. Hell no, never will be that dumb over any man, Alexis and I have somebody. Does he take me for a fool? My face had a serious mug on it. I grilled both bitches.

The two of them attempted to ruin my life for different reasons. Juelz and Kairo. Why would I be ok with being in the same space as your wife and Giselle? Does that make any sense? It's levels to this shit, just off the strength that he thought it was ok to bring me here with those two, they're going to regret even being in my space. I pushed Kairo out of my way and looked at Alexis.

"You know what time it is Alexis."

The two of them better be ready to throw hands. How in the fuck are y'all on this plane and they brought us too? We approached Giselle and Tyra, and we started tagging them both. I ran up on Giselle first I wanted to get her, because I missed the opportunity at my house. I knew all about her stalking Juelz, Mrs. Simone told me she had to lay hands on the stupid bitch. I socked her in the head one good time. Alexis took it from there.

I didn't give a fuck about Giselle's daughter crying her bitch ass daddy shouldn't have brought us here. She should've closed her eyes. Kairo and Free had a hard time breaking the fight up. Tyra and Giselle attempted to fight back, once they noticed Free and Kairo attempting to break up the fight. They were no match for Alexis and me. I was already heated that I didn't get to tag Mia's ass, but I'll see her again and she'll feel me.

"Journee stop that shit, it's not that serious. It's not what you think," he argued.

"Nah, it's not what the fuck you think. I don't want to fucking be here."

I kept on tagging Tyra's ass, just because this stupid ass nigga thought it wasn't serious. I'm tired of niggas and bitches trying me. It's not even about Kairo, it's about quit being dumb behind a man that doesn't want you.

Shit, he might do want her, but I don't want him, and I don't want to keep company with you like everything is cool, because it's not. You played and didn't give a fuck. If you would've kept that bitch happy I still wouldn't know.

I don't care how much you had or what type of wealth you obtained by being with her. I didn't need it I could live without it. I don't mind working for what I want. Nobody gave me shit. Everything I have I got it myself. Whatever he did was extra, and I didn't really need the extra.

Giselle's daughter was screaming like somebody was killing her trifling ass mammy, that's the only reason we stopped her cries was fucking with my ears. Kairo had the nerve to pick me up.

"Don't touch me."

"You don't run shit," he argued and pushed me in the seat.

"Keep your hands off me. I fucking hate you I don't even like looking at you. You fucking disgust me."

"I love you too, I don't give a fuck how you may feel right now, but I love you and nothing will change that."

I wish he would just leave me the fuck alone it's that simple you can live happily with your wife. Tyra was looking shocked bitch this is what you want. I don't want him I've been over him ever since Juelz has come back into the picture. Juelz had a hold on me like no other. I can't wait to make it back home to him. I know he's going crazy.

I'm pissed that I rode with Alexis now. If I would've never brought my ass to Skeet's party and stayed at home like Juelz told me too. I wouldn't even be in this fucking situation. It is what it is because Alexis would've ridden with Alonzo she wouldn't be here either. God doesn't make any mistakes, things happen for a reason. I know he didn't bring me this far to leave me.

The only thing I could do now is keep the faith and hope my plan to kill Kairo and make it back home to my family would work out just fine. Juelz and I were just about to start a life together and this bullshit happens. Minor setback for a major comeback. I'm making it back to the states. Jueleez needs me and I need her. I can't stand to be away from my baby more than two days. I must get this plan on the road and make it back quick.

Chapter 6

Kairo

Journee was really trying a nigga. I've been real patient with her. I will not tolerate her fucking disrespect at all. She refused to look at me like my word isn't law, that's ok because I'm the only nigga that she's going to see for a while. I gave her everything she wanted. She acted like that shit wasn't good enough. The moment she agreed to be my lady she was stuck with me.

I don't agree with her fighting Tyra and Giselle that was uncalled for. She thought she was hurting my feelings telling me she wanted Juelz. It's was funny because she wanted something that she wasn't going to be able to have anymore. They have the right to be here rather she liked it or not.

I made a mistake, I was young, and I could've handled the shit better, but I didn't. The moves I made set us straight financially, where did she think the money came from? I brought her a house every year. She vacationed like a queen, and Jueleez had the best of everything. I wasn't her biological father, but I treated her like she was my own. She didn't have to work if she didn't want too. Julissa's was just something to do.

I knew she would leave me and I didn't want her to leave. I'm tired of talking about this shit. It was weeks ago, let's move on so we can make up, fuck that little break up. The real question was, could I get over the fact that she got pregnant by him so quick and she's about to have his baby. Nah I couldn't accept that shit. I just couldn't, when I met her she was pregnant. It took me over a year to fuck.

I wanted Journee to have my first child years ago, but she wouldn't give me one. I tried to get her pregnant, so many times and that shit didn't work. She claimed she wasn't ready but as soon as this nigga steps back in the picture. She has her legs cocked up and she's pregnant. That's another reason I kidnapped her, I thought she was better than that, we haven't even been broken up two months, and you're already screwing the next man in a house that I brought you.

I knew she was fucking him that's why I was so angry with her when I pulled up because it was written all over her face. She walked to the door and her nipples were hard. She smelled like him and she had passion marks on her neck. Her hair was untamed, she looked the same way after we fuck.

Giselle

Ugh, I guess the saying is true to be careful what you wish for because you just might get it. I wanted Free to leave Alexis for years because I was selfish and the thought of having two men at once intrigued me. One thing about tables they always turn and let's not speak on karma because I've gotten that in the worse way.

Everything backfired on me at once. I nursed Free back to health an attempt to go back after Juelz. Juelz mother beat me senseless and left me for dead. That was the first wake up call for me. Free came home and found me unconscious, and he was livid, but that still didn't stop him from trying to get back with Alexis.

He thought I was stupid I knew he was stalking her because I followed him and watched him follow her. If I watched Juelz, what would make Free think he was excluded. He was sloppy with his shit. He was obsessed with her.

I'm tired of fighting these two girls and being their personal punching bag when shit don't go their way. I didn't ask to be here either. Free never got the ok from me about having Alexis here with us.

He danced around the subject hinting about it. I was against that, I may be a lot of things, but I wasn't born yesterday. Last, I checked he was my side nigga and he finally moved up to Plan B by default.

Why would I want to be in the same room with Journee and Alexis of all people? I hate those bitches. I despised them. Journee fucked my man, and I've been fucking Alexis's man for years. My track record isn't squeaky clean, but I'm not a whore, my pussy is just as tight as Journee and Alexis. I've only been with three men.

See I was caught off guard by Journee and Alexis they tagged me a few times and wanted to fight me in front my daughter, as soon as they get comfortable on the plane. I'm smacking the fuck out of the both of them. I have my Vaseline and I'm ready to go.

Journee is a mother herself I can't believe she would stoop that low and fight me in front of my daughter. I would never do that to her. I'm low, but not that low. Free called himself checking on me to see if I was ok. I spit in his face. You know I'm not ok with this shit.

Bitches were laughing at me now I'll have the last laugh. With or without Tyra I'm going get the satisfaction of smacking the both of those bitches. I move better by myself anyway. If she would've never wanted to go to Journee's house after Kairo divorced her.

I would still have Juelz. I lost my nigga because this basic ass bitch couldn't let go. I was still salty because she aired my shit out, and it wasn't her place to do so. I've been looking at her funny ever since. Before she even aired her shit out she put me on blast

I'm cordial with her, but I keep my distance.

Tyra

I'm not here to start any shit. I know I'm not a fighter I still love my ex-husband. When Journee shot me in my face and left me for dead, Kairo was there for me. I couldn't even look in the mirror Journee ruined my face. He took me the hospital to make sure I was ok, and he paid for all my surgeries, he said it was my fault, and I should've never gone to her house.

I didn't know that it would end up like that, but it did. My parents were furious they wanted Journee dead and Mrs. Farrah was pissed she helped nurse me back to health and whipped up a few African remedies to mask some of the scarring.

I still have some scars on my face from the knife wound and the bullet to my face. I had plastic surgery done. I still needed another layer of skin added to my face. I thought she was going to kill me. My life flashed before my eyes when she pressed the gun toward my cheek. Tears flooded my eyes I just started crying out of nowhere. I placed my hands over my face. I didn't want anybody seeing me crying.

"Tyra are you ok," he asked.

"I'm ok." I sniffed.

"Look at me, get your hands off your face. I'm sorry you're still beautiful despite your scars don't cry. I got you," he explained. I looked at him it's not that I didn't feel beautiful, I just didn't like this situation.

I wanted him, but he still wanted her. I started crying again his words didn't soothe me. He picked me and hugged me. I wanted my husband and I know he was only doing this because I was upset.

"Kairo do you think I want to see you hug and console this bitch," she yelled and kicked him in his back. She reached around him and smacked me in the face.

"Can you stop?"

"Keep your hands and feet to yourself Journee," he yelled.

"Make me motherfucka," she yelled. I could feel the spit fly out of her mouth. I know Kairo felt that shit too.

"I'm sick of her putting her hands on me, this isn't going to solve shit."

"Are you talking to me Tyra?"

"Yes."

"I'm not going to stop shit Tyra, for the record, I don't give a fuck about you and your husband. I don't want to be here. I don't fuck with married men. I've been taken against my will. The only thing I want is my daughter and my baby daddy. Until I get both of those you and this motherfucka gone feel me."

"He kidnapped you?'

"Yes, we've been kidnapped."

"Kairo what the fuck is going on here?"

"Don't ask me any questions I'll tell you what you need to know and when you need to know it," he snarled and gritted his teeth.

"What's the big secret? Why is she here?"

"Look I already told you don't ask me shit. I do what the fuck I want. Do I need to have the pilot to turn this fucking plane around and you can get off and fend for yourself?"

"Are you serious?"

"I'm dead fucking serious, the less you know the better."

I'm confused what was his motive. If she didn't want to be here why would he bring her here? She's made it very clear that she doesn't want him. If she didn't want him anymore why would he continue to pursue her?

Giselle looked at me and I looked at her. I couldn't read her facial expressions. I could tell that she was just as confused as me. What have we gotten ourselves into? I'm not down with no sister wives shit. I love Kairo with all my heart, but some shit I'm not willing to do. He couldn't have me and Journee.

Kairo and I have been partners for years and when he made business decisions he normally ran shit by me. I'm confused by this whole situation here it blows me. What part of the game is this?

Chapter-7

Giselle

The two of them bitches have finally gotten comfortable on the plane. I watched them both nod off. You could tell they were more like sister's than best friends. I laughed devilishly just thinking about smacking the fuck out of these hoes tickled me. These bitches ain't no better than me. Journee was hoe, and Alexis was too.

I waited until they were dozed off good. The plane took off over an hour ago. I approached them both. I smacked Alexis first she jumped up out of her sleep. I smacked the fuck out of Journee next. They both woke up and starting cussing and raised up out of their seats. I had some scolding hot water in a cup ready to burn their fucking faces if they thought about jumping me again.

"Y'all hoes got one more time to fight me in front my daughter and I'm going to black the fuck out. I owe y'all that. Take that fucking L like I have. If the beef is that serious we can throw hands anywhere, but not in front of my child. Would you like for me to fight you in front of your daughter Journee?"

"Giselle, don't ever in your fucking life smack me while I'm sleeping. Anytime we've ever had a disagreement you initiated it. So, don't act like you're holier than thou. Everything that comes to you, you deserve that shit. If it makes you feel better to smack somebody while their sleep, then I'll let you have that. I never have to catch somebody off guard," she argued and sucked her teeth.

I don't care what she thinks, you were going to feel me whether you were asleep or wake. I felt Alexis staring a hole in me.

"Alexis you'll be all right, one lick won't hurt you, I've taken plenty."

"You better shut the fuck up talking to me before I tag you again and not give a fuck about your daughter sitting next to you, I'm a disrespectful ass bitch."

"I wish you would, Free you better get this bitch."

I looked at Free and gave him an evil look, he better check that bitch about showing her ass in front of mine, and I'm not tolerating it anymore.

"Hi, can I ask y'all a question please?" My daughter asked.

Lord, please give me the strength because if Journee or Alexis says some off the wall shit to my daughter I'm going straight in. I grilled the fuck out of both of those bitches. I love my daughter as much as Journee loved her daughter. I might not have been the best mother, but I'm learning. I'm doing a lot better than I've done lately. I would protect my daughter at all cost.

"Sure," Journee smiled, Alexis rolled her eyes and turned her head the other way.

"Why don't y'all like my mommy and why do y'all keep hitting her?"

"Kassence, it's not that I don't like your mommy, we had a disagreement and it was never resolved. I'm sorry for hitting your mommy in front of you." Alexis, just rolled her eyes, see that's the shit I'm talking about.

"Can I have a hug Journee?"

"Sure Kassence." Journee smiled and gave my daughter a hug. I don't know why Kassence likes her. Tyra was furious as fuck. Kassence sat on Journee's lap and played in her hair. Journee wasn't a bad person I just hate that Juelz was so in love with the bitch. I guess they deserved each other because Lord knows I fucked him over, but he fucked me over first.

Kassence felt safe with Journee, she felt comfort in her. I could tell the way she laid up under her. It's funny that she didn't want her daughter around me, but Kassence is smitten with her. I'm sure I wouldn't hear the end of this from Tyra, but I don't give a fuck. Instead of her running up behind Kairo and crying every five minutes she needs to boss up and stand her ground.

I'm tired of getting my ass beat and dragged I'm all cried out.

Journee

Kassence was amazing too bad her mammy ain't shit. I see why Juelz loves her adorable self. Juelz wouldn't admit it, but I know he missed her. I would never stop him from seeing her or taking care of her because she was his daughter for eight years and all sudden she's not.

She makes me miss my daughter so much, she's the sweetest little girl and super smart. Giselle has her dressed so pretty. I understand why Alexis was acting the way she was acting, but Kassence didn't ask to come here. She was innocent in this whole situation. I couldn't put myself in her shoes because I haven't been there.

I know she doesn't care for Free or Giselle right now, and her feelings are hurt, because she always wanted children and Free always said he wasn't ready, but he has an eight-year-old daughter. Alexis couldn't stand the thought of being around her. She got up and left and moved two seats back. I looked at her, and her eyes were blood shot red.

Out of all the times, I agree with Giselle I should've never put my hands on her in front of her daughter. I would never want Jueleez to see any of this shit. I feel bad for fighting in front of her. No child should see their mother getting beat up. Kassence was tired I rocked her to sleep, she fell asleep in my arms.

Giselle wasn't off the hook she's one bitch that would never get the pleasure of saying that she smacked me, and I didn't do shit about it. You're a damn lie I wouldn't get her on the plane because her daughter is here, but as soon as we land, and her daughter is out of sight. I'm laying the fucking smack down. I laid Kassence down and I walked back to check on Alexis.

"Best bae you good?"

"No Journee I'm not, the only reason I didn't light fire into Giselle because of her child, and I understood where she was coming from."

"I know, you know I'm here for you."

"Niggas ain't shit, he keeps staring at me."

"He's guilty and I'm sure it's eating his soul."

"I know if I kill Kassence mother and father, you and Juelz will have to take care of her."

Alexis joked to keep from crying Free knows that he's wrong for all this shit. He just couldn't take the high road and move on. What goes around comes around and he'll get his.

Chapter- 8

Khadijah

If it's not one thing, it's something else. I already had an attitude I feel like Mrs. Simone jinxed my sister, bitch don't wish my bad on my sister. Journee is all that I have besides Khadir and Jueleez. Excuse my language but damn as soon as she said that shit. Something bad happened to Journee and Alexis. Right now, I'm not feeling Smoke or Juelz. I couldn't get this Apple watch to work for shit, that's another reason why I'm pissed off and my hormones are all over the place.

I was playing the blame game if Juelz would've never brought that bitch Mia to the party on some get back shit. Journee would still be here. His little plan didn't work the two of them still ended up together.

"KD, what's wrong?"

"Smoke you already know how I'm feeling right now."

"KD you can lose the attitude I haven't done shit to you. Don't ever in your fucking life think that you're about to start fighting just because you want too and you're pregnant with my child. You got me fucked up."

"Whatever." I walked off from Smoke because I'm not a child and you can't talk to me any kind of way and expect for me to be cool about it. I'm not Journee and he's not Juelz. I'm hard headed and I do what the fuck I want, and not what I can. He grabbed my shirt and I looked at him like he was crazy.

"Khadijah don't play with me, I don't know what you're used to, but I'm not that nigga I'm a different breed. I'll handle you how I see fit," He argued and pushed me up against the wall in Nikki's house. I started crying into his chest.

"KD stop crying. I got you I got us. Journee and Alexis are going to be all right. You're pregnant with my child, trust me when I tell you that your sister is coming home. Journee has a lot of heart and Juelz will die before he lives without her." I was tired, Smoke carried me into the guest room, because I couldn't stop crying and he didn't want me to stress the baby out.

***

Smoke and I laid down in Nikki's guest room. I laid on his chest. We haven't heard a word from Journee. Juelz was going crazy him and Alonzo both. I could hear them arguing downstairs. My Apple Watch alerted me that I had a message. I raised up and grabbed my watch it was a message from Journee.

I tapped Smoke on the shoulder real hard, so he could wake up and see. I grabbed the watch and the charger, so I could plug it into Nikki's TV or computer. I ran downstairs so I could tell Juelz and Alonzo.

"Journee sent me a message on my Apple Watch," I yelled.

Juelz, Alonzo, Nikki, and Skeet ran into the family room to see what was going on. I hooked the watch up to the TV and we all sat back and watched the video. Alexis did all the talking and she showed us a video she looked fine. Her hair was all over her head. We heard Journee in the background talking. Juelz mood had shifted a little Alonzo was still hot. They're going to Ethiopia. I had access to all of Journee's personal information and properties. They all can sit around here and look crazy, but I'm heading to Ethiopia fuck all this shit.

"I'm going to Ethiopia I'll see y'all soon." I walked off and prepared to leave.

"Khadijah don't fucking play with me, you're not going anywhere and you're pregnant with my child. Let Juelz and Alonzo handle this shit. If they need back up, then Skeet and I are going."

"Smoke you don't understand."

"Make me understand Khadijah why in the fuck you think that you're about to up and go to Ethiopia without thinking shit through."

"She's all I have, and I can't lose her."

"Khadijah, stop crying do you actually think that Journee's going out like that? She's calculated."

Smoke will never understand why I need to do this. I know I'm pregnant, but I will be just fine. I know Journee has a plan, but

I have one too. I'm my sister's keeper if a nigga thought they could take my sister from me than it's going to be some consequences.

I just wanted Journee to be happy she was finally about to experience that with Juelz until Free and Kairo ruined it. My sister has been strong all her life she's everybody's back bone and I wanted to be her back bone for once, that's why it's so important for me to go. Smoke couldn't relate because he has his mother and father. Journee doesn't have anybody I'm all she has.

Juelz

Journee sounded good, but that shit didn't move me. I lost her once and I refused to lose her again. I needed Khadijah to stand down and do what the fuck Smoke say's because I got this. Kairo isn't an average ass nigga and he'll be expecting us. He has something that I want and I'm sure he's preparing for my arrival, but I'm going to get him when he least expects it.

I know one person who can tell me everything that I need to fucking know.

"Alonzo and Skeet ride with me."

"I'm going also."

"No Smoke, you're not, you need to watch Khadijah."

Smoke couldn't roll with us because Khadijah is up to some shit. Nikki knew better she wouldn't move unless Skeet gave the ok, but Khadijah hard headed as fuck she's always been that way.

"Where are we going?" Skeet and Alonzo asked.

"Giselle's." They didn't say anything, they just nodded their head in agreement. I didn't kill Giselle for more reasons than one. I knew this bitch would come in handy. I wasn't in love with her. I always had love for her even though she fucked me over on numerous occasions. I'm still fucked up that Kassence isn't my daughter because she's all that I knew for a long time.

Giselle watching me love another woman that's not her would kill her slowly.

***

We finally made it to Giselle's house. Skeet took the back, me and Alonzo took the front. No one answered immediately. I kicked the door open and yelled for Skeet to do the same. Giselle's place was spotless nobody was here. Alonzo searched upstairs, and I searched down stairs. I went in the garage Giselle's mustang was inside and a Purple Bentley coupe with her name on the back. I felt the hood it was cold It hasn't been driven.

I grabbed my phone to call Giselle to see where the fuck she was at.

She didn't answer, but her phone was ringing normally. I called her again and she cleared me out. I called back again, and she was whispering.

"Hello," she whispered.

"Bitch where the fuck you at?"

"Watch how you talk to me."

"Get that base out your voice and answer my question."

"I'm on my way to Ethiopia and I got your bitch with me."

"Oh, it's funny? You think this shit is a game, I will kill your fucking mother and grandmother now play, put my bitch on the phone now."

"Juelz, you wouldn't do that would you?"

"Don't cry now, I will do what the fuck I said I would do."

"Juelz, I don't have anything to do with this, hold on I have to sneak and do it. They don't know that my phone works."

"Do it now, stop fucking crying."

Giselle knew not to play with me she might not have feared Free, but she feared me, and I would act on killing her mother and grandmother.

"Here she goes make it quick before you get me killed."

"Journee, what the fuck did he do to you, is my seed straight?"

"Juelz, I love you. He hasn't done anything yet. Our baby is good, don't let Jueleez know what's going on."

"I love you too, I'm coming to get you do you hear me?"

"Her signal is fading but Khadijah has access to everything that you need." Damn the signal faded.

I felt better to hear from Journee myself. Giselle might not be in on it since she gave Journee her phone to speak with me. It still doesn't make sense. If Free was fucking with Giselle what would he need Alexis for? What was Kairo's motive?

"Alonzo and Skeet man let's clear it I just talked to Journee and Giselle."

"Did you hear from Alexis?"

"No, but we need to speak with Khadijah. Journee said that Khadijah has everything we need. Giselle is in Ethiopia too."

"Man, this is some crazy ass shit. If Giselle is in Ethiopia too why did Free take my bitch?"

"I don't know that's what I'm trying to figure out, I don't think that Giselle is in on it."

Kairo was a lot of shit more than what Journee mentioned she was affiliated with. I taught Journee how to hustle and I hope she wasn't tied up in his drug business. If he took her to Ethiopia than more than likely it's a possible the FEDS could be looking at her too. I couldn't wait to look at this paperwork to see what was going on.

Journee isn't a rat but Kairo maybe worth more to her being dead than alive. No face no case, they have a case against him and she's been with him for the past eight years they can easily hit her with conspiracy. My mind is in overdrive just thinking about if she got caught up in some bullshit with a fuck nigga. Journee was smarter than that.

Chapter-9

Giselle

Juelz was really in love with Journee. I hate to admit but he was. I guess she's what he's been missing. I broke them up for as long as I could. I guess when somethings meant to be it'll be. I could hear it in his voice that he was serious about killing my mother and grandmother behind this. I wonder would true love ever find me?

I didn't have anything to do with Kairo kidnapping Journee. Free told me that we were going to Ethiopia for a few months to kick it and chill. I was perfectly fine with that. I needed a vacation. The first thing I did was un-enroll Kassence from school because he said, she'll attend school in Ethiopia for a few months. He told me he had to handle some business for his mother since his father died. I knew Free killed his father because of what happened between him and Alexis.

When we went to visit his father's body at the funeral home before they sent his body back to Ethiopia. I stepped out for a minute to use the bathroom. I watched him from afar, he was smiling like a chest cat watching his father lying dead in that casket. I knew then that something was wrong with him and he killed his father.

Free lied to me we may have been here for business, but he brought Alexis here for pleasure. The moment kidnapped rolled off their tongues. I knew something was up, but I'm tired of a nigga disrespecting me. After Juelz and his mother beat me senseless. I thought about settling down with Free and leaving Juelz alone.

He walked in here hand and hand with her that was too disrespectful. Yes, we met each other on the strength that he had a girl and I had a nigga, but once everything was out in the open. I thought we were official. I see Free had another plan. Tyra can continue to be dumb if she wants too. My days of being dumb over a nigga are over. I know Journee has a plan I want in on that shit.

I'm over Free and Juelz, it's somebody for everybody and I'm sure it's someone for me. I guess it's true the same way you gain them is how you lose them. When I met Juelz, he was a single man. Free was in a relationship and so was I. We've always been open with each other up until today. I can't believe he pulled this shit on me.

Alonzo

I'm not an emotional ass nigga. I'm not the type of nigga to do relationship type of shit. I don't have feelings. I wear my heart on my sleeves. I never knew my mother or father. My grandmother raised me, but I learned my life lessons in the streets and in the trap. Alexis and I never put a title on what we have, she knew what it was, and I knew what it was too. Yeah, I fuck off in the streets from sunup to sundown but at the end of the night, I'm coming home to her.

I feel bad as fuck because our last conversation wasn't pleasant we were arguing about the shit that she did at Skeet's party's now I'm regretting the fuck out of my choice of words.

I heard everything that Juelz said but he didn't see what I saw. I haven't heard from Alexis or got the okay that she was okay. You know what they say you'll never miss a good thing until it's gone, and I feel like I'm missing my good thing. I'm a real nigga and I don't bend or fold.

I'm going to do everything in my power to bring Alexis back home. She has me feeling something that I've never felt, and I can't control this shit. I'm a street nigga and I don't fall in love. Alexis has a nigga ready to change his ways, and it might be too late.

"Get out your feelings." My partner Juelz yelled, breaking me out of my thoughts.

"Put yourself in my shoes, you've heard from Journee I haven't heard from Alexis we were beefing something serious before she pulled off in traffic. I said some shit that I shouldn't have."

I knew some niggas who fucked with some niggas off Summerhill that knew Free and Kairo, they pushed heroin and choc for them. I grew up with them. I made a few calls they had their ears to the street to see if they could find out anything.

Nobody was talking, but they heard Kairo and Free were going to be out of the states for a while and their cousin Efren was running shit. I had a name now I just needed a face, too bad for Efren he was going to have to see me, whatever bullshit his cousins have going on he was the first one that was about to pay because Free took a bitch that didn't belong to him. Alexis was up for grabs, and I'm the nigga that grabbed her.

Alexis

I'm so fucking furious right now. I'm shaking, and nothing can keep me calm until I had the satisfaction of handling Free. Anytime I get upset I have to walk away because I'm liable to kill somebody. I couldn't wait to get to Ethiopia to meet these chicks that Journee knew so I could orchestrate this plan to kill Free and take my ass back home.

I'm missing Alonzo like crazy. We had an intense argument, it was so bad because of the shit that happened at the party. He said some shit that he shouldn't have said, and I did too. Just the thought of not being able to see him again fucks with my mental. I could see myself being with him. I swore I was good on men for a while. Alonzo is different, we're one in the same.

My mind is so fucking blown right now did I fucking miss something? What the fuck did I miss, because Journee and Giselle were never cordial what did they go in the back of the plane and do? I could've sworn I saw a smile on Journee's face.

Don't get me wrong two wrongs don't make a right. I couldn't change or take back what I did. Free having a daughter on me was cool I accepted it because I didn't have to see it. To sit here and see this shit with my own eyes for more than an hour it's breaking me. I had to close my eyes to keep from crying, normally it helps but tears seeped through my eye lids. My emotions were all over the place and they had a mind of their own.

I grilled the fuck out of Journee as soon as she made it back to her seat. Journee is the sister I never had, we're more than friends. I know she'll never switch up on me. I couldn't be cordial with Giselle because she was cool with fucking with a man that she knew had someone and she didn't think it was wrong.

Giselle thought she really won after Journee beat Tyra's ass on my birthday. Reality finally set in, she could no longer have Juelz. She accepted that only for a minute because she had Free, and you're the same bitch that was screaming it still leaves me single. I just wonder how does it feel to be with a man and he's still running up behind his ex.

I'm sure it sucks Juelz and Free have both done the same thing to her. Cheating is only fun when you don't get caught. I'll make sure to ask her that after Journee explains herself. It takes twenty-four hours to get to Ethiopia and we have a long fucking flight. I have nothing but time to get some shit off my chest.

***

Chapter -10

Journee

Damn It felt good to hear Juelz's voice, but I was a little salty why was he calling Giselle's phone? She was staring a hole in me the whole time I was talking him and telling him that I love him. I crept back to my seat like nothing happened. Kairo was looking at me and Tyra was sitting on his lap, this nigga disgusts me. I nudged the Alexis, she looked at me.

"What the fuck is going on?" she asked grilling the fuck out of me.

"Calm down, you know my loyalty lies with you. The only thing me and her have in common is we both have a daughter that's it. Giselle's phone works and Juelz called looking for me. I think he's coming to Ethiopia." I had to whisper because I didn't won't Kairo or Free to hear me.

"Oh, I'm just checking, where was Alonzo."

"Alexis, I heard him in the background."

"I miss him, but I don't trust Giselle I'm sorry."

"I miss Juelz too. Do you think that I trust her? She never cared for me."

"Good because you know, you always look for the good in a person."

"Alexis, don't start."

I couldn't wait to get to Ethiopia, so Alexis and I could sit back and fucking plot. I noticed Giselle walked behind us. Alexis and I instantly squared up ready to box this hoe out. She walked up to me and whispered in my ear she wanted in.

"Giselle, why should I trust you?" I whispered.

"Because this nigga played me."

"Giselle, you got played seriously?" I gave her the side eye and Alexis laughed.

"Yes, why would I agree to come to Ethiopia with the two of you and we don't like each other, and we've had a physical altercation? I maybe a lot of things, but never would I agree to any of this shit. A man can cheat, but he's not going to cheat in my face and think I'm going to accept it."

"Giselle, loyalty is priceless and I'm not sure if you have that quality. Only time will tell. Actions speak louder than words.

"You'll see."

"Journee, she does make sense. She may be a lot of things even though she can't fight she does have heart," Alexis admitted.

"I hear you."

I wouldn't say I'm a bad judge of character. I can normally read a person. Giselle didn't have bad intentions. The only time I got a bad vibe from Giselle is when she came to my mother's house years ago. Even a few weeks ago I could tell that she wasn't lying about not coming to my house with no bullshit.

She was just with Tyra and a casualty of war. To be honest she could've hung up the phone when Juelz called and been in her feelings and cut her phone off. She put her pride aside and gave me the phone. Khadijah has everything that Juelz needs if he wants to come to Ethiopia a. I really don't want him to come. I think Alexis and I can handle it. Jueleez needs him there with her.

I'm curious now I want to know why Kairo and Free kidnapped us on some get back shit. It's something else that's going on. As soon as I reach Ethiopia I need to find out what's going on. Even Tyra is confused about what's going on. It's something serious because I could tell in Kairo's tone. It's hard for me to even pretend that I like Kairo if even for a minute because he can't be trusted. He's lied for years with a straight face, and what would make now any different. Everything you do in the dark comes to the light.

I looked up and he was approaching me and Alexis.

"Can I speak to you for a minute alone?"

"I don't think that's a good idea Kairo."

"Journee I'm not asking you I'm telling you and I don't want to make a scene."

"Kairo, are you threatening me? I'm pregnant and I can't stand the smell of cheap perfume. I'm about to throw up. I need you to take that shirt off and hand it to Tyra before you and I can speak about anything." He threw his shirt at Tyra, and grabbed my hand and led the way to the back of the plane. She was pissed.

"What's up Kairo what can I do for you?" He just stood there and looked at me.

"Journee."

"Kairo."

"I got some shit going on, and I need you to chill out with your mouth and you putting your hands-on Tyra. I understand you're upset, but she's been through enough and she has to look in the mirror every day at her face that you fucked up."

"Kairo good bye leave me alone. I thought you had something serious to say. You caused all this shit here, but I need to chill out. You kidnapped me I could be at home with my family, but I'm here because you can't accept that I moved on. Last I checked I was chilling."

***

We finally made it to Ethiopia. Kairo and Free had me and Alexis treated like prisoners. As soon as we got off the plane we were thrown in the back of a Mercedes van with two guards. I looked at Alexis and she looked at me.

What the fuck is really going on? Alexis started crying again, as soon as they slammed the doors to the van. I don't have time for this shit.

"Damn are you pregnant too? I should be the one crying. I'm pregnant and I have a daughter who needs me. Look bitch I need you to boss the fuck up. I need you more now than I ever needed you in my life. We have to execute this plan and get back home, this is where your Marines training comes to play."

"Journee what if I can't come through?"

"I don't do what if's. I don't mind standing ten toes down by damn self I've always done it. It's not even about Juelz. It's about Jueleez, Khadir, and Khadijah. My family is everything to me."

"All of this is too much for me."

"Calm down take a deep breath. Relax, I'm going home it doesn't take all day to kill a motherfucka and take my ass back home. I'll be home in seven days. If I have to fuck Kairo and kill him in his sleep that's what I'm going to do."

"Everything just happened at once, but I got you. I got us. I just need to know exactly how you want to do everything."

"I will I just need to figure out how we're going to get down South to Somalia to meet up with Pure, Majesty, Eboni."

"Don't use your pussy. It's caused enough damage."

I didn't even respond to Alexis she knew better. I was just glad that we finally made it to Ethiopia. I need to shower, change clothes, and get started. I would be as nice as possible to Kairo. He has a little plan or something, but I have one also.

***

Kairo

Umm hum, I know y'all heard about me. Don't believe any of the shit you heard about me unless you heard it from me. I'm not a bad person. I just made some mistakes along the way due to greed and wealth. I'm working on myself. I kidnapped Journee to protect her. I could've gone about it differently, but I didn't she wouldn't agree to come on my terms. I'm a take charge type of nigga so I can take charge the best way I know how.

She had to come to Ethiopia because of the FEDS and my indictment. Journee was my business partner. All our dealings were legit, but I cleaned dirty money using our businesses. The FEDS were already looking at me, but they didn't have anything concrete to get me on. I have a federal drug case and I also have a case for racketeering.

Everything was going smooth and Journee wasn't a part of the case that was built against me until she started dissolving her name off our businesses and listing her real estate for sale. One of the federal agents working the case noticed it and immediately had a case pending against Journee as a co- conspirator. I don't think Journee would fold on me, but given our history lately, I couldn't take any chances.

No face no case. I have Ethiopia under lock. I control everything moving and going. I decided to flee back home because my country wouldn't comply with the United States at all. The only way the FEDS could catch me is unless I was on US soil. The FEDS have been building a case against me since March of this year. They had enough evidence against me to hide me for the rest of my life.

I've always been a calculated nigga. I had a few FBI agents and judges on the payroll. Mia the little chick that I had fucking with Juelz who use to be a stripper she's an undercover FBI agent. She gave me play for play. I was a few steps ahead of the FEDS all my money was in foreign banks and offshore accounts.

They could seize the homes and my business's, but I would burn all that shit down to the ground and collect my insurance check before I ever let the government reap the rewards of my blood, sweat, and tears. I wasn't at home because I didn't want to be at home. I wasn't at home because I refuse to let the FEDS catch me in my home.

I didn't have the time to explain this to Journee the day we had plans to meet with our attorney. We had an intense argument I was already under a lot of stress. I just wanted her to do one thing, and that was change her clothes that's it.

Our attorney was going to explain everything to her. It would've been foul of me to leave her in the States in the blind and face the FEDS on her own. I did what I had to do. I couldn't leave Tyra I had to bring her also.

Her brother is the reason we're on the run now. He got caught doing a drop, he was so dumb and not checking his surroundings. When he dropped off the work and grabbed the cash and dropped it off at the stash house. The FEDS have the transaction on tape. I'm the only person coming in and out of the establishment. Hell, no I couldn't leave Tyra behind because she will fold under pressure and flip. I know Tyra maybe in her feelings because Journee's here. I had to protect them both to secure my freedom and Journee's.

Tyra's parents want Journee dead because she fabricated the story of what happened. If they even looked at Journee wrong I would kill them. I'm in a fucked-up situation. I must protect Journee and my ex-wife. I must protect my brother in his family. I couldn't leave my brother in the states he was my right and left hand. The FEDS would hold him to get to me. He has a family to take care of.

Alexis is here because she ran the family business that dealt guns and arsenal. She was ahead of the arms control department. She had the hook-up with military weapons. Tyra's brother sung like a bird when the FEDS picked him up. I have somebody on the inside about to shut him up for good.

Free couldn't risk Alexis folding on him so he had to snatch her up. Everybody's Freedom is at risk, we didn't want to fuck with each other, but we had to due to our business ties. I'm not saying that Journee or Alexis would fold, but do to everybody's recent history we couldn't be sure. Giselle didn't have any business ties with us. Free wanted her and his daughter here. I would explain everything to Alexis and Journee later.

I'm not sure how to explain it to Tyra because her brother is in the FEDS and she hasn't even mentioned it. For that reason alone, I believe she has a hidden agenda. I find it funny as soon as I wanted a divorce the FEDS pulled up on me, to think that I even had a thought of taking her back.

Chapter-11

Giselle

We finally made it to Ethiopia Suddenly a bad feeling came over me. I've never been her before it was beautiful, but I couldn't enjoy it. I had a feeling that something bad was about to happen and for some reason, I couldn't shake the feeling. Tyra was smiling looking like the devil. Journee and Alexis were thrown in the back of a Mercedes van. We were in a Maserati SUV. Tyra and Kairo sat up front.

Free and my daughter and me were in the back. We pulled off from the Airway strip. As soon as we stopped at the light and turned the corner. A gray Lexus pulled up and started shooting the van that Alexis and Journee were riding in. I started crying the gun fire was close to me I knew they were dead. I grabbed my daughter and held her close.

Kassence was screaming her lungs out. Tyra was laughing as soon as the gun fire ceased. I jumped out of the SUV to check on Journee and Alexis.

"Tell them bitches Tyra said welcome to Ethiopia bitch."

"Tyra, you did this?"

I slammed the door shut and ran to the van to make sure they weren't dead. I'm low but not that low. I don't think a bitch could get me that mad to orchestrate a hit out on somebody. I see now she can't be trusted. You have crossed the line twice. It won't be a third time. Bullet holes and shell casing were everywhere. The van door swung open.

"Are y'all ok? I thought y'all were dead."

"Thanks for checking on us. So, I'm guessing we were the only car that was hit up? Tell Tyra she must come better than that. Her husband makes sure I'm bullet proof. It's not a bitch walking that can touch me. I'm one bitch that she doesn't want to shoot it out with."

"Journee, I have nothing to do with her, and what she has going on."

"I believe you." I'm relieved to know that they were ok. I walked back to the SUV got in and slammed the door shut.

"Don't ever walk out of the car again, unless I tell you too."

"Free I'm not your fucking child. Unlike you, I have a heart. No matter what bullshit we have gone through. I don't want to see nobody die."

Tyra just grinned I wasn't even going to tell her the van was bullet proof. I guess everybody knew except Tyra and I. I'm not feeling this shit at all.

Tyra

Welcome to Ethiopia! I see now Giselle can't be trusted. This is my country and if Kairo thinks that Journee can walk around here untouched after what she did to me, he has been sadly mistaken. As soon as I saw those bitches walk on the plane. I sent a message back home. I wanted that bitch offed she was in my territory now.

My parents wanted her dead, but Kairo was to pussy whipped to do it. I knew Kairo was on the run from the FEDS who do you think tipped them off? When Kairo threatened to leave me months ago, and take the majority of everything. I had to secure me. I wanted him gone months ago, but things didn't plan out the way I wanted them too. Kairo was smart, but I was smarter he thought by fleeing to Ethiopia he couldn't be touched.

I'm a US citizen all I must do is contact the FEDS and let them know that I've been kidnapped by a fugitive on the America's Most Wanted List and for the right price my country would expedite Kairo he's worth millions and I'm not talking one or two. I wanted it all. Try me and see I may not have as much as I would if we were still married, but if I can't have him nobody would but the United States government.

He had the nerve to grill me. I'm sure I would hear his mouth as soon as we got to our destination. I knew as soon as we're behind closed doors he's going to lay hands on me. I wonder where he was staying. We have a house here and he has a house built with that bitch. Yes, we're divorced my family didn't know that. I wanted to keep it that way.

      I closed my eyes and laid back and enjoyed the ride this trip back home could make us or break us. Lord knows if Kairo ever found out that I'm a government informant on his case and I was testifying against him. He would kill me.

Juelz

Two days have passed by, and I haven't heard from Journee. I called Giselle's phone and it was going straight to voicemail. I'm meeting with Khadijah today to get the information that I needed to go to Ethiopia. My mother had Jueleez, she called me a few times wanting me to pick her up.

Jueleez is a smart girl she's been asking for her mother. Journee told me not to tell Jueleez what was going on. I told her that her mother and Alexis were on an all-girls trip vacation. She was cool at first until she started calling Journee's phone to speak with her and her phone went straight to voicemail.

My daughter was upset she knew that something was wrong. Journee normally FaceTime's her every day, and she hasn't heard from her in a few days. I hate to lie to my princess, but damn I don't want to see her upset.

"Jueleez, I have something to tell you. Promise me you won't to get upset at what I'm about to tell you. It's only temporary."

"Yes, daddy I promise."

"Your mother went to Ethiopia, she had to handle some business with Kairo and her phone doesn't reach over there, but she'll be home soon."

"Mommy has us a house in Ethiopia. We have a computer she can FaceTime or email me."

I was honest with her, it didn't matter what I said, she knew her mother had a way to contact her. Journee never told me she had a house in Ethiopia.

"Jueleez, have you ever been to Ethiopia?"

"Yes, daddy four times."

I'm curious now I need to get over Khadijah house immediately. I need access to everything it was time that I step foot in Ethiopia to see what the fuck was going on. If you had a house there, you got me fucked up. If you think for one minute that your about to be alone with him and my child in another country and I'm babysitting, you have another thing coming.

"Let's go Jueleez were going over Khadijah's."

"Yay!"

My mind is in the gutter right now. I know Journee wouldn't do that to me but how could I be so sure. She's done that before after all that we've been through I hope she wouldn't fuck It up because she's alone with him.

Chapter-12

Khadir

It feels good to be at home despite the circumstances. Regan and I are staying at my mom's house. I haven't even seen Khadijah because I had my eyes and ears glued to the street, to see what's up with Kairo. So far, I haven't heard anything. His cousin Efren was running shit. My pops told me that the FEDS were looking for Kairo and he was wanted. He wanted to make sure I didn't have any business dealings with him. I brought a few guns from him years ago.

I have to many bodies on my hand to use the same gun twice. I'm mad as fuck at Khadijah right now because she's pregnant. How does she think that she can run shit and she's pregnant? The life we live is dangerous and Khadijah can't run her fraction of the business. I didn't mind running Atlanta and Florida. I know how Khadijah thinks and I don't want her to think that I'm stepping on her toes.

Since she's pregnant and dating all our business are foreign to her, but that's cool because I want her to be happy and live her life because if a nigga ever tried my sister in this game. This thing we call life would be non-existent.

"Baby are you ready to go meet your sister, what if she doesn't like me?"

"Yeah, I'm ready. She'll love you because I do. Khadijah better not be on no bullshit. I know how she is that's another reason I haven't gone over there. She would ask me a hundred questions and swear that Regan wasn't good enough for me. I would hate to have to make my sister cry because she's overstepping her boundaries.

***

Regan and I finally made it to Khadijah's house. Regan was nervous. I grabbed her hand, so I could assure her that I had her. I rung Khadijah's doorbell and she swung the door open.

"Hey Khadir, I missed you." Khadijah reached out for a hug.

"I missed you too Khadijah."

"Who is this with you? You know I don't like thots at my house or where I live."

"Khadijah go head with that shit. Reagan isn't a thot she's the love of my life. My woman. Move out the way and let me in this bitch." I pushed passed Khadijah. Regan and I walked into her house hand and hand.

Khadijah

Khadir thinks he's grown. I'm his big sister. I run shit. He knew I didn't allow females knowing where I live. I've never heard of Regan until today. I guess he has the sneaky gene just like Journee.

"Excuse me, Regan, I'm Khadir's older sister let me introduce myself since his rude ass can't. I swore I taught him better than that. You look sneaky and I'm keeping my fucking eye on you."

"Khadijah this is Regan. Regan this is Khadijah the annoying sister I told you about, who thinks she's my mother, but she's deceased may God bless her soul. I'm sorry Khadijah but I didn't tell you about my woman because I knew you would act this way."

I can't stand Khadir sometimes, that's here nor there. We needed to talk business our businesses and Journee. Juelz was coming over with Jueleez to get the paperwork that Journee had regarding her house in Ethiopia.

"Can we talk in front of her?"

"We can but you don't have too if you don't want to."

"Ok cool, but no offense to you Regan, but I don't pillow talk with nobody, not even my nigga. Let's go to my office." Khadir and I went to my office to discuss business and Journee of course. No shade to Regan, but I don't know you. I would kill a bitch dead fucking over my brother. Khadir looked at me and I looked him, shit I didn't say anything wrong. I loved him.

"Khadijah, you know you're wrong for that shit. Let's get straight to business no more queen pen shit for you. I will handle your portion of the family business. When you got pregnant that was a game changer."

"Khadir you can't count me out. I'm barely even showing."

"I'm not cutting you out. I need you to chill out, you can't move like you use too. I need muscle. You have a baby growing inside of you. How in the fuck are you going to be my muscle? Does Smoke know you push weight and you count keys by the boat load? Does he know you have stacks stuffed inside of your mattress and a lean factory in the basement?"

"No."

"That's what I thought Khadijah. Don't fight me on this shit. Being pregnant comes with emotions. Emotions will get you fucked up in this business. Ain't no room for fuck ups."

"How am I supposed to get paid?"

"Khadijah I'm never going to shit you. I got you."

"You better."

Khadir and I chopped it up. He wanted me to cook him some steak nachos. I did as I was told anything for my little brother. Regan helped me in the kitchen. She was a cool chick. My doorbell rang I told Khadir to get the door.

"Uncle Khadir." That voice belongs to Jueleez. Juelz has finally arrived. Jueleez ran up and hugged Khadir. She missed him. I missed him too. The only person missing was Journee. I looked at Juelz and he looked at me he gave me a faint smile.

"Auntie Khadijah has my mommy called you from Ethiopia, she has a computer and phone at our house over there?"

"No Jueleez she sent me a message on my Apple watch. I'll have her to call you." Jueleez was a smart little girl. She was her mother's child, she knew Journee would never leave the country without taking her.

"Jueleez, I made some steak nachos. Come and get you some while your uncle Khadir and I speak with your father."

"Okay, auntie."

Juelz

We made it to Khadijah's house. Khadir and who I assume was his girlfriend was there. I forgot all about Khadir, he wasn't even that tall the last time I saw him. His name is ringing bells out here in these streets. I heard he was the man to see if you wanted coke or heroin for seventeen five.

Journee told me he was in college playing basketball. Ok, he's playing basketball all right. I'll leave it that. She'll find out sooner, or later. Khadijah thinks that she's so slick too. Smoke was on to her. He knew that she was doing something illegal. He couldn't confirm exactly what it was, but he was ready to bust her out. I find it funny the two of them were dibbing and dabbing in the drug game.

It was a given because of who their father was Big KD. Ms. Julissa was so hard on Journee it was crazy, but I respected it. I understood where she was coming from. I hope Jueleez never does that.

"Khadijah where's the paper work? What's up Khadir?"

"Dang Juelz I got it." Khadijah gave me the paperwork of Journee's house in Ethiopia. Damn the layout was nice as fuck.

"Juelz, I want in. If you're going to Ethiopia I'm on the flight. Khadir was ready.

"I got you." I really didn't want anybody going with me to Ethiopia but me and Alonzo. Kairo kidnapped the wrong one. He needed to feel me. I let him slide the first time. You took matters into your own hands, you knew she was with me. My child needs her mother. Everything that you've done was personal.

I chopped it up with Khadir and Khadijah for a few minutes. Jueleez asked could she stay with them. I didn't have a problem with it. I need to chop it up with Alonzo and Skeet anyway. I had the floor plan of Journee's house and Kairo's house. I couldn't go to Ethiopia unprepared. I had to assemble a team of hittas to go with me. Kairo is a calculated nigga and I'm even more calculated and smarter. I called Alonzo, so he could meet me over Skeet's he answered on the second ring.

"Meet me over Skeets"

I needed Journee and my son home ASAP. It takes twenty-four hours to get to Ethiopia and normally you must stay for a month. I was killing everything moving and I planned on coming back home within seventy-two hours. The only problem I had was how was I going to get these guns through security.

Alonzo

Juelz hit me and told me to meet him at Skeets. He had some information that was valuable. I had my ears to the street to see what was going on. I had two of my nigga's Skill and Dre following Efren to see If we could snatch his ass up to get the drop on Free and Kairo.

Efren had shut the shop down and switched up the whole operation because of the FEDS closing in and having a case. My cousin Asia worked at the Federal building in Atlanta. I had asked her to check out Free, Kairo, Journee, Alexis, Tyra, and Giselle nothing made sense. Asia was digging for me with Kairo's case being Federal and sensitive she had to move differently.

If you weren't assigned to the case, you weren't supposed to look at it because your credentials would be logged in the file. She was in the process of getting some credentials for surveillance to access the case. She advised her boss that she received a tip that's how she could gain access. Skill and Dre dropped me off at my car, so I could get up with Juelz. Alexis has me doing shit that I normally don't do. She better be the one because I'm not getting any younger. I hope to see her again soon, so we can clarify some shit.

***

Damn Asia must have something for me! She sent several PDF attachments to my phone telling me to look and delete asap. I sped to Skeet's house I couldn't wait to look at this file.

It had to be serious Asia reminded me three times to get rid of the phone afterwards. I made it to Skeet's house in about thirty minutes. I pulled up and hopped right out. Juelz was just pulling up perfect timing.

I missed Alexis like crazy and it hasn't even been a week I guess it's true you don't miss a good thing until it's gone.

Nikki

God doesn't make any mistakes. I never question his actions, but damn why Journee out of all people. My girl has been dealt a bad hand since the beginning of time. She lost both of her parents at an early age. Every obstacle that has been thrown at her she has overcome. I'm sure this time would be no different. I miss our morning talks. Little Skeet and Nyla miss their Godmother so much

Lord knows that my mother is going crazy if Juelz and Alonzo don't handle their business soon she's going to take matters into her own hand. I need to speak with Journee myself to know that she's ok. Kairo was a heartless ass nigga. I saw how they did Alexis's truck on the news it looked horrible.

I need the two of them to call me immediately. Journee has been to Ethiopia plenty of times and she has called me every day. This time is different I didn't even notice that I've started crying. In my bedroom, I have a bay window. I sat in it and just stared out the window crying my eyes out with my phone in my hand. If only we would've killed them, we wouldn't be here today.

"Baby what's wrong?"

"I miss her."

"We're going to get her back I promise you."

"This shit ain't fair Skeet."

"I know but Juelz isn't about to play fair. I'm going with him to Ethiopia."

"I want in."

"Look, Nikki, I know you do. I won't risk my wife for nothing in this world. Trust me and my niggas. We're going to bring them back. Stop crying, Juelz and Alonzo are downstairs. Go get sexy for me and I'm going to take you anywhere you want to go to clear your mind." Skeet wiped my tears and placed sweet kisses all over my face. I swear I love him so much, he's everything to me. We've been going strong for so long.

What we have is special I wish everyone can experience it. When it's your time it's your time. Timing is everything and I'll be patient for now and pray for better days. Life is funny it has a way of knocking you down and picking you back up. I just hope and pray that Journee doesn't fall back in love with Kairo, he will charm the fuck out of her. I want her with Juelz they were made for each other.

I know him. I hope and pray Alexis hasn't killed Giselle. I miss my girls so much ugh I hate just thought of it. Khadijah's running around here selling more drugs than a CVS pharmacy and she thinks that I don't know. I wanted to tell Journee last week, but that shit slipped my mind. I went by her job about three weeks ago to surprise her with lunch and a massage courtesy of me.

I approached the front desk and asked for Khadijah they said that she hasn't been working there in about two months. I called Khadijah to play it off she said she was on vacation meet her the house. I pulled up at her house and got in the car with her. She had two duffle bags full of hundreds stacked tall. I asked her where did she get all his money from she said she was counting for her daddy.

I knew that was a lie because she couldn't even look me in my face. I could tell that she had been trapping all night because of the clothes that she had on, and her hair was unkept. I tried to walk in her house, she wouldn't let me in. She said it's a mess I knew right there she had something to hide. I let her do her though.

I wish Journee was here, so we could bust her together. Khadijah always wanted to be in the streets so bad and she didn't have too. She was making a big mistake keeping her work where she laid her head at. I still haven't seen Khadir yet. I saw his car parked down Ms. Julissa's the other day. I started to stop, but I kept going. I swear Khadijah and Journee will be the death of me. I'm too fine to die at an early age. I got something for Khadijah she would never see this coming.

I called Smoke and he answered on the first ring.

"Aye, I need to speak to you face to face about some shit."

"Cool I'm around the corner from your house I'm about to pull in five minutes." I smiled just thinking of the plan that I've come up with.

Chapter-13

Journee

Ugh, I was so furious when the van was shot up. I couldn't remember if Kairo had a bullet proof vest and choppers still in the floor. I looked under the floor, sure enough, they were there. I wanted to open the door and bust back on whoever.

If a bitch shot me in the face they would never live to tell about it. I see now I'm going to kill Tyra I've never caught a body before, but this would be my first one. I knew this was Tyra's doing.

"Fuck that, driver pull this damn van over. Call Kairo I need to speak with him." The driver did as he was told. He pulled the van over and let me out. I grabbed the AR from the ground. I walked up To Kairo's SUV I approached the passenger door. It was open I pulled Tyra out and I pistol whipped that bitch.

"You want to fucking get at me bitch let's go." I gave this bitch some more work, in case she forgot. I slammed her into Kairo's truck I didn't give a fuck.

"Journee chill out with that shit, you didn't get shot."

"Kairo, I don't give a fuck. A bitch is going to respect me period. Tell this hoe to stay in her fucking place and we wouldn't have any issues. I kicked her in the face and walked off.

***

I'm still heated about this shit. Every car that Kairo owns is bullet proof, so for somebody to do that they didn't know any better. Tyra didn't want to play with me. I don't care about this being her country. I would body her and bury her here. The van finally came to a stop. I looked at Alexis she was in a daze, her mind was in over drive. The van door swung open. It was Kairo and Free. I looked out and we were at Kairo's house.

"Take me to my house."

"Journee, I need to talk to you about some important shit."

"That's fine I need to call Jueleez. I haven't spoken to her in three days." Kairo gave me his phone so I could Facetime my princess. She answered on the first ring.

"Hey, mommy I miss you. I knew you would call me."

"Hey, baby I miss you too. I love you and I'll see you soon. Where are you?"

"I'm at Khadijah's, Khadir is here too."

"Let me see Khadijah and Khadir." Jueleez did as she was told. Kairo was looking crazy I didn't care. I would take his phone and call Juelz and Nikki too. I chopped it up with Khadijah and Khadir telling them to stand down. I would be home soon, and I'll call them when I can. I told Jueleez I love her and I would call her tomorrow because I would. Kairo asked for his phone back. I had to call Nikki first then he could have his phone back.

"Hello."

"Yeah mane, what it do, Shawty? I heard you missed your girl and shit. They can't hold a real one down forever."

"I'm trying to tell you. Free, Journee Leigh and Alexis until they free I miss y'all so much."

"I'm trying to tell you. You know I had to call you. Where's lil Skeet and Nyla? Tell them I love them."

"They're outside playing. Where's Alexis put her hot breath ass on the phone." Alexis and Nikki chopped it for a few. Kairo and Free were becoming inpatient.

"Nikki, we have to let you go but tell Juelz I love him and I will see him soon." Kairo snatched his phone out of my hands and hung up on Nikki.

Kairo

Journee was so disrespectful she wanted me to know how much she loved him. True enough we weren't together, but you didn't have to rub it in my face. It was all good though. I'm not even going to trip right now. I took Journee to her house. Alexis went with her. Free couldn't fool me no matter how much he said he didn't give a fuck about Alexis and him didn't want to be with her he did.

I knew he killed my father. I knew Alexis wouldn't fold because she worked for the government and she would get more time if she betrayed the country that she served. Free knew that shit too Alexis took her oath seriously.

"What are you thinking about? Journee let me guess huh?"

"Free, stay out of my business. Worry about yours. You're wrong for doing Alexis how you did her."

"You wrong too. We're two wrong niggas. Fuck Alexis she'll never make it back home fucking with a nigga like me."

"Let her live you already killed my father behind some pussy."

"Oh, so you know. If I killed my father because he disrespected me, and he didn't have any loyalty to me. Why would I spare her?"

"You know what Free I'm not even about to go there with you. I'll get up with you later." I couldn't even argue with Free right now; my mind was on Journee. I doubled back around to her compound. She needs to fucking respect me. I love her, and I'll put that shit at the back of my mind and she'll really hate me. I used my hand print to get in. I scanned the compound for Journee I couldn't find her. I walked upstairs to find her, and she was in the tub. She was relaxing with her eyes closed. I tapped her on the shoulder with so much force. She looked at me and closed her eyes shut.

"Journee stop fucking disrespecting me. I don't care how much I love you I will fucking hurt you."

"What more can you do to me that you haven't already done? You can leave and I'm removing your handprint."

"Look at me when you're fucking talking to me."

"Kairo, I fucking hate you and that's a strong word that I use lightly. I hate to even look at you." Journee's words hurt a nigga soul, she really meant that shit.

"You miss daddy, don't you? Look me in my face and tell me you don't love me, and I'll let you be."

"Kairo do you really want to hear me say it."

"I do."

"I don't love you at all! You abandoned me when I needed you the most. I could never love a man that's married and openly lied day after day and played me. I prayed to God that he would take any love I ever had for you out of my heart and he's done that.

I appreciate everything that you've ever done to me and for me, and I'm forever grateful, but love doesn't live here anymore." I appreciate Journee's honesty but some of the shit that rolled off her tongue I refuse to tolerate it and accept it. The game has changed and I'm sick of her thinking that she can say what the fuck she wants to me without it being any consequences. I've apologized to her too many fucking times and I'm not kissing her ass anymore.

I jacked her ass up out of the tub and threw her over my shoulders. She was soaking wet. She kicked me and punched me in the back of my head. I threw on the bed and grabbed her face roughly and placed my hands on her neck.

"You don't think that I'll fucking hurt you physically? I don't give a fuck how you may feel about me, choose your fucking words wisely, when you're speaking to me. I did what I had to do to protect you. I didn't hurt you on purpose."

"Why do you want to hurt me Kairo? I ain't did shit to you but love you. I'm at fault for loving the wrong nigga. You fucked me over, you were still married to her. You got me out here looking like a fool."

"Yeah, I want to fucking hurt you. You didn't even give me the chance to explain myself. We haven't worked through any of our issues. I've been with you longer than I've been with her. I don't want to throw eight years away, but you're forcing a niggas hand. Tell me what I have to do to make it right?"

"Kairo just leave there's nothing that you can do."

"No, I'm not leaving. I have some shit to tell you that's beneficial to our future."

"Really, talk."

"I'm wanted by the FEDS that's the reason that we're out here. They're trying to hide me for the rest of my life."

"What does that have to do with me?"

"Everything you're my business partner and you've dissolved all of your assets with my name attached. It's suspicious and they're charging you as a co-conspirator to my case.

I brought you out here to protect you. I couldn't let you go down with the FEDS by yourself." Journee smacked the fuck out of me.

"Kairo I didn't have anything to do with this shit. I have a daughter and another child on the way. I need to turn myself in and clear my name."

"Journee it's not that simple." Journee's whole mood has changed, after that. I left I bumped into Alexis on my way out.

Chapter-14

Alexis

Damn I hated to be a fly on the wall. I was going to check on Journee because I heard her and Kairo arguing from downstairs. I had to check and make sure he wasn't hurting her. The argument between the two of them was so intense it sent chills through my body.

"You can come in now Alexis. I don't keep secrets." Journee yelled I guess she could hear my foot steps in the hall way.

"Are you ok?"

"No, I'm not. Did you hear what the fuck he said?"

"I did."

"I sold our assets, so I wouldn't have to deal with him or have any ties with him at all."

I felt so bad for Journee I really do. I could tell that she was about to break down and cry. I don't need her upset and she's pregnant with my Godchild. I put it on everything I love if Free got me caught up with the FEDS because I assisted him with the Arms and Arsenal Division affiliated with the Hussein Mafia fraction of the business.

I swear to God I will mix some poison and kill him. I always told Free that I didn't want to be dope boy's wife. I would help you expand your business and kill any competition, but if your business ever interfered with my way of living it's a wrap. I know Free better than he knows himself and he's in his feelings about a lot of shit. I need him to enlighten me on what the fuck is going on.

"Journee can I see your phone?" I called Free and he answered on the third ring.

"We need to talk, make your way over here now."

"Alexis watch your fucking tone before I hurt you."

"Not if I don't hurt you first." I hung up on him. I already found two butcher knives in Journee's kitchen. I would stab the fuck out of Free if he got me caught up in his shit. I would make sure he bled out. I got something for his ass he handled me like a man.

I was in my feelings about this shit, but the old Alexis is back, and I'm savage when it comes to bodying fuck niggas. Free trained me and that can be a good thing or a bad thing. The worst thing that you can do is go to war with a bitch who knows how you move. I was his strength and he was my weakness. For his sake and not mine I better not be affiliated with none of this shit.

I headed down stairs to make me a fruit salad. Free needs to bring his sorry ass on.

"Alexis, you're up to something?" Journee came into the kitchen and joined me.

"I am depending on this conversation that I have with Free." I ran down my plan to Journee if I'm caught up in their bullshit. We need to head down South to Somalia immediately and link up with Journee's friend's, so I could assemble a team together and get me and my best bae home. I got a pen and pad and started putting my plans in motion.

Journee and I continued to chop it up for a while until Free finally decided to show up he was high as fuck. He banged on Journee's door like he was crazy. I had a knife sitting by the door. We just looked at each other. He walked right passed me and sat on the sofa. I broke the silence.

"Free do you have anything that you want to tell me?"

"Alexis, why are you looking at me like that?"

"Free I'm not trying to go there with you just answer my question?"

"Come here, sit on my lap because I need you calm when I tell you this."

"Free, I'm not doing all of that. Just tell me damn."

"Alexis come here! I know you and when I tell you this I have to hold you in place because I know how you are and I can sense how you're going to react." Ugh as bad as I didn't want too. Free knows me, we've spent eight years together. I sat on Free's lap he wrapped his arms around my waist, and grabbed my hands and placed them on his chest. His touch used to do something to me. It doesn't even move me a little bit. Whatever Free had to tell me it had to be serious because he was huffing and breathing heavy trying to get his words together, he finally cleared his throat and started to speak.

"Alexis, we got caught up, we've been through it all together. I didn't do anything wrong. I'm not a reckless ass nigga. I'm flashy that's it. A nigga got jammed up and folded on the whole Hussein Mafia operation."

"What does that have to do with me? It ain't no we. It's just me, we ain't together." He whispered in my ear and gave me the rundown of what happened. My heart dropped, and tears formed in my eyes. I started shaking and held me in place. I couldn't believe any of this shit I'm hearing. I started to speak but he cut me off. He could continue to tell me more.

"Free, Tyra is in on this shit too. I know she is I feel that's why I'm pissed."

"I got you, trust me."

"Yeah ok. My trust is fucked up." I walked Free to the door, he grabbed my face and kissed me. I didn't kiss him back because I know where it would lead too. I tried to close the door on him. He placed his shoe in between the door and forced me against the wall.

"Stop Free, please don't do this. Don't do what you did to me to Giselle."

"This doesn't have anything to do with her. I want you. My hearts belongs to you and that'll never change. I know I haven't been the best nigga to you lately, but let me make it up to you." Now isn't the time for Free to be in his feelings, his timing is off. Journee walked toward the living room and interrupted him. Thank God.

Journee

If it's not one thing, it's something else, of course, I was ease dropping on Alexis and Free.

I needed to know what was going on. I knew Kairo wasn't telling me everything. He was in his feelings and I was in mine too.

Don't get me wrong I loved Kairo with all my heart and I would never wish bad on him despite what we've been through, and the charges we're facing. I'm stuck in a difficult situation. Kairo didn't tell me any names because he kept his street dealings away from me. The less I knew the better.

Free and Alexis relationship was different than ours. Free told Alexis everything she was his muscle and he was hers. Free told Alexis that Tyra's brother was the reason we're all fucked up. Kairo was smart, but damn you're stupid. If the real reason he stayed married to Tyra was because of the business relationship between her family and his family. As soon as you wanted out and the divorce, everything started to crumble.

Tyra and her brother set Kairo up. She tried to kill me because of him. I just don't understand why Tyra's brother is still breathing. I can't stay in Ethiopia and be on the run. I'm finally looking forward to giving Jueleez a two-parent home with her mother and father. I refused to let Kairo and the FEDS bullshit charges stop me from doing that.

I need to be home in a week I couldn't stand to be away from Jueleez and Juelz for too long. I crave him. Kairo is forcing my hand. I wanted to kill him, but damn does he really deserve to die. I have to think hard about what I want to do because Juelz would be coming here soon if I wasn't home within a week.

***

Sleep finally consumed me four hours later. I tossed and turned all night. One would think that I would be sleeping good sense I'm at one of my homes. I had a hot bath and a hot meal, and I was able to relax, but that was far from the truth. I thought about Juelz and Jueleez all night. I reminisced about him. He was so good to me.

I had a computer in my house, but I'm not sure if Kairo is tracking every move or not. I handled my hygiene I planned on cooking me and Alexis a big breakfast before we headed to make some plays. I heard my doorbell ring. I wasn't expecting anyone. I marched down stairs to the door I opened the door and it was Giselle and Kassence. Hmm, this is a nice surprise Kassence gave me a big hug.

"What are you doing here?"

"I told you I wanted in." I looked at her and rolled my eyes. Kassence grabbed my hand and wanted me to pick her.

"You want some breakfast?"

"I do."

"Giselle, I was talking to Kassence."

"I'm speaking for her. We're hungry and I don't eat African food."

"Yeah whatever, you need to stop popping up at people's compounds."

"Whatever we're passed that now. I don't know anybody here. I don't trust anybody but you. Where's Alexis I smelled her cheap ass body spray on Free last night."

"Look, Giselle, chill out ok." Giselle was comfortable around me and her daughter was hooked on me also. Alexis stomped down the stairs and marched into the living room and gave me the side eye. This could go one or two ways.

"Journee Leigh, why is she here?"

"Alexis, I'm here because I want to be here. Is that a problem with you? Last, I checked this was Journee's compound and not yours. She welcomed me and my daughter in."

"Journee am I missing something? I'm confused on why she's here with us and not Tyra. No new friends."

"Look Giselle and Alexis both of y'all need to chill, especially you Giselle. I guess we have to form some type of bond, because of the cards that we're being dealt. Giselle, it's not easy for us to sit here and act like everything is peaches and cream with you because it isn't. We can't change the past only the future. I'm over it."

"Journee, do you have a room where Kassence can chill, while we all talk?"

"Sure." I grabbed Kassence and took her to Jueleez room, so we all could talk. Lord be with us when we have this conversation because I can already look at Alexis and tell it's about to be some shit.

Chapter-15

Giselle

"Let me say this. I'm so tired of explaining myself. We've all made mistakes. Trust me I've learned from my mistakes. Journee, you slept with a married man for years no shade, and Alexis you let Mr. Hussein suck on your cat for a few racks. The two of y'all ain't no better than me. I know I haven't been the nicest person to the both of you guys, but y'all haven't been nice to me either.

If you want to be technical about everything Journee, Juelz was mine first you started fucking with him while he was with me. He didn't break things off with me until after he brought you the Mercedes truck. He was still sleeping with me and laying his head at my condo.

Alexis, when I met Free he said he had a girl, but they were broken up at the moment. We both had a situation. I tried to cut him off on a numerous of occasions, and he made it real hard. I never wanted to have his child. I didn't trap him, he trapped me. Do you know how many abortions I had? I was about to have an abortion with Kassence and Free found out. I think he had somebody following me.

He pulled up to the clinic where my appointment was scheduled, he pushed passed the doctors and nurses and pressed a gun to my forehead and dared me to kill his baby while he watched, and he would kill me if I killed another one of his kids. He's crazy I avoided him for weeks because I was terrified of him. He showed up at my mother's house and threw me in the trunk because I was avoiding him." I cried.

"No shade Giselle, but I don't want to hear anything else about you and Free. I'm sorry you went through that with him, but his behavior comes with him, that's just who he is. I can't honestly sit here and act like I can be cool with you, and you fucked my fiancé and has his first child something that I didn't give him. I can't overlook that, it goes against everything that I stand for. Can I be cordial with you, yes that's about it."

"What about you Journee, how do you feel?"

"Giselle, let me be honest with you. I didn't know that Juelz was with you when we first got together. We just happened, as soon as I found out you were a factor, it was a wrap."

"What about now Journee?"

"I didn't pursue Juelz because I know you were in the picture. We didn't cross that line until he officially called it quits with you."

"I appreciate that."

"Since we're keeping it real and trying to move forward and form some type of bond. Don't ever in your fucking life, leave your bed at 4:00 am because your man is doing something. Nine times out of ten he is, but we didn't do anything." Journee explained. I knew it was her all along. It felt good to finally get everything up off my chest. I don't know about Alexis, but I could see me and Journee moving forward. We prepared breakfast, well I cut the fruit and they did the rest because I didn't cook. Journee's compound was beautiful it looked better than Tyra's.

Chapter-16

Journee

Normally I'm pretty good at judging people. I don't think Giselle is on any slick shit given her track record. I have to consult with Alexis first because her opinion matters to me. One thing that I would never have to question is her loyalty, and if she's not cool with it, then it's a wrap. Her word is law. Giselle and Kassence finally left and went to meet with Free and Kairo's grandparents that was perfect.

I decided to sit outside in my garden and just observe the atmosphere. It was beautiful, and the flowers smelled perfect. It was about 82 degrees. My mind was heavy and cluttered. I had a lot of stuff to figure out. I heard footsteps behind me. I looked over my shoulder and it was Alexis, just the person I wanted to see."

"Hey boo, how are you, what do you think about Giselle?"

"You already know how I feel about her. Trust is earned not given. She can talk a good game all day, just because we're in Ethiopia ain't no Kumbaya shit over here. Prove it that you're not on any fuck shit. Don't tell her any of our plans at all.

I'm ready to move around, let's go I think I'm pregnant too my breast are really sore." Alexis ain't never lied. Julissa didn't raise a fool. I thought she was pregnant, but I didn't want to say shit, she has been in her feelings too much lately.

I walked around on the side of the compound. I had a shed where I kept my mopeds stored. We were headed to town to visit the local shops, so I could use their internet to email Juelz everything that was going on.

***

We made it to the coffee shop and bakery, in about thirty minutes. My neighbors didn't know I was home. They stopped us on our way out asking for Kairo and Jueleez. We could've made it sooner, but Alexis kept complaining about the heat.

She better chill out before Free finds out that she's pregnant and get a witch doctor over there to check her out. The first stop me and Alexis made was by the tea shop called TeeBee's it's located in the little strip mall.

I wanted some freshly brewed coffee earlier and a coffee cake, but Giselle stopped by and I don't drink coffee in the afternoon.

It was obvious that Alexis and I wasn't from around here, oh well. All the shops that were on Front Street were very nice and upscale. It gave you the Bistro feel. Majority of the Ethiopians frequented that here, were on the main strip instead of the ones in the back that were rundown. I wanted some spicy Ethiopian Beef Suya and spinach later. Juelz would kill me if he knew I was eating this spicy ass food.

I'm sure Kairo and Free had somebody watching us. I gave Alexis the name of the shop that I was about to sneak off too, so she could follow suit. It was called Cameroons. It was run down on the outside but on the inside, it was immaculate.

It was plush Gold and a rust red. It had nice African art and it smelled good. It was a nice bar and lounge. Pure and Eboni's moms own it. I crept into Cameroons and as soon as I opened the door. Momma Edith greeted me, she was my mother away from home. I loved her dearly.

"My beautiful Journee Leigh what do I owe the visit and where's Jueleez Monroe?"

"Dang ma, can I get a hey how are you doing or something?"

"No, I haven't heard from you in months, and I had a dream that you were in danger, my child." She grabbed my face and placed a kiss on my forehead after she observed me.

"I'm sorry ma you know how life is. It picks you up and kicks you back down. Jueleez is with her biological father. Kairo kidnapped me and brought me here. I'm pregnant again By Jueleez's father. I need to get in contact with Pure, Eboni, and Majesty."

"Her father finally knows about fucking time. I'm glad Jueleez has finally got the chance to meet her real father. Ugh, Kairo kidnapped you? I like him, but not for you. He's selfish just like his mother and father. Why are you pregnant so soon my child? You couldn't wait to spread your legs for him. Would you like for me to take you to Somalia, or would you like for them to come here?"

"Ma why are you so hard on me? I thought you missed me. He trapped me. I prefer to go to Somalia."

"You let him." Momma Edith and I chopped it up for a while. Alexis finally showed up I introduced the two of them they hit off pretty good. I grabbed Edith's computer and sent Juelz a long email. To my surprise, he emailed me back immediately. He wanted me to FaceTime him. I responded back and told him that I couldn't she didn't have a MacBook. I wanted to see him as bad as he wanted to see me.

I could FaceTime Jueleez all day I trusted Kairo to a certain extent. I knew I couldn't FaceTime Juelz from my house Kairo's jealous ass would cut my internet connection. Juelz and I went back and forth about me and him FaceTime each other. He didn't give a fuck about my connection being interrupted. He wanted to see me. I hated to argue with him about something so small, but I would FaceTime him later. I wouldn't be able to sleep if he was mad at me.

Juelz

A few days went by and I still haven't made my move yet. I became irritated by the minute I had to make sure everything was calculated perfectly. Africa is a foreign country and I couldn't pull up in Africa the same way I move around here. I had some shit in motion.

Journee has been calling Jueleez every day and letting her know that she was good. She couldn't call me from her compound because if Kairo found out about her sessions he would be on some bull shit fuck him.

She emailed me from a coffee shop with instructions on how to get to Somalia and who I needed to contact when I got there. I don't trust people, but she said that three women by the name of Eboni, Pure and Majesty they worked for her, and if I needed to make some serious moves they would help. I took down the information and I would reach out to them in a few days if she's not able to get down there sooner.

I told her she can do what the fuck she want's and he can deal with the consequences later. He doesn't run shit a real nigga doesn't have to kidnap females. Kairo had a lot of shit going on that Journee didn't know about, she only revealed a few things to me. We went back and forth about her FaceTime me I needed to see her anybody can send an email I wanted to make sure that she was good.

Alonzo wanted to see Alexis too. Hopefully, she can make it down there soon because a nigga getting tired of sitting around here without her and Jueleez is getting very inpatient. My mother is getting on my last nerves asking when is she coming home. She misses her daughter in law. My momma crazy I can't believe she like Journee but I'm glad she does.

Journee better call me when she gets home, or I'll be FaceTime that laptop my damn self to see what the fuck is really going on. Khadijah is running Smoke crazy too with her dramatic ass.

Journee

We finally made it home after being gone all day. Momma Edith got in touch with Pure and tomorrow she's sending a car to pick me and Alexis up and take us. I decided to cook me and Alexis some dinner I went upstairs to my room, so I could FaceTime Juelz. He answered on the third ring. He was laid on the bed licking his lips, he knew what the fuck he was doing. His shirt was off, his beard was trimmed to perfection and his gray sweats pants had the bulge in his pants on display. He has no business wearing gray sweat pants if I'm not around.

"I'm glad you're not being hard headed and decided to listen to what I had to say."

"Juelz, don't start. Where's my baby?"

"In your stomach."

"My other baby Jueleez."

"She's with my mother."

"I miss you."

"I miss you too."

"You look handsome. I'm going to burn those sweatpants when I get back."

"Why?"

"You know why."

"Whatever don't nobody want me but you anyway."

"Yeah that better be the case, Giselle and Kassence came by today."

"So, who else came by?"

"That's it."

"You have four days to get home if not I'm coming to get you. Alonzo and I. Where do I need to fly too?" Juelz and I stayed up on the phone all night long, talking about everything up under the sun. I missed him the only thing I wanted to do was lay up under him.

I miss the way he held me. I don't want to have to kill Kairo, but damn I have to do what I have to do. It's killed or be killed. The only thing that mattered to me was my family. I love Ethiopia and I know once I take care of Kairo I would never be able to come back here. With Kairo out the picture, there wouldn't be a case. Tyra has to go too. Juelz didn't care that Giselle and Kassence came by. Damn, why couldn't Kairo just leave me in the states to fend for myself?

***

I was so tired from staying up on the phone with Juelz all night. I realized what time it was because my alarm went off and instantly woke me up out of my sleep. I wiped the sleep out of my eyes and glanced at the clock. It was 7:00 am. Pure said the car would be here to pick us up at 8:00 am. I ran down the hall to wake up Alexis up. She was already up and dressed, and I could smell the breakfast cooking.

"Good morning, hey to you too. Thanks for dinner last night."

"Alexis, I'm sorry I got caught up with Juelz we stayed on FaceTime last night until the laptop died. I miss him so much."

"Bitch I know I miss Alonzo too, I need to see that laptop tonight to FaceTime him. Go ahead and get dressed and I'll fix your plate. I think I'll hit Alonzo up now." I ran back upstairs to handle my hygiene. I had the water temperature turned up extremely high. The water felt like fresh rain up against my skin too bad it couldn't wash away the pain. I finished taking my shower quickly because time wasn't on my side. Lord knows that I need to eat. My wardrobe consists of African attire. I had a few track suits, shorts, skirts, jump suits and maxi dresses.

I wanted to be comfortable because Lord knows what Pure, Eboni, and Majesty is up too. I opted out for track shorts a fitted tee and some fresh white air maxes. I oiled my body with fresh coconut oil. I braided my hair last night in three French braids. I took my braids down so my curl pattern in my Afro would look nice. I coated my lips with a nude coconut African lip balm.

***

As soon as we finished stuffing our faces and laid back on the sofa. Our car arrived, our driver knocked on the door and asked for us. Pure was really showing out. The distance between Ethiopia and Somalia was about four hours away. The car was taking us to a boat dock. Taking a speed boat, we would be in Somalia in two hours. Alexis and I observed the scenery. I haven't seen Kairo in two days.

I'm sure today would be the day I saw him. We arrived at the boat dock and it was, it was still early in the morning the sun was peeking through the clouds. It was hot and humid. The only locals at the boating dock were fishermen and shrimpers. We boarded the speedboat, and placed our life vests on and sat back and enjoyed the ride. It was few other people on the boat with us, a few guys, three females and an older woman with a child. The older woman looked at me and Alexis and asked.

"When do you have your babies?" She had a thick African accent.

We looked at each other and asked her was she talking to us. She nodded her head yes. I told her that I was the only one that was pregnant, and I was due in June of next year. She said that Alexis was pregnant also she had a pregnancy glow to her. We continued to talk to the older lady she was headed to Somalia also.

***

We finally made it to Somalia two hours later. I was hungry my stomach was growling. The boat docked at a local Fish Pub, you could smell the fresh fried fish as soon you walked off the doc. Pure, Eboni and Majesty were waiting for us as soon as we stepped off the boat dock. Pure and Eboni ran up to me and hugged me. I introduced them to Alexis. Majesty just grilled the fuck out of me. I walked up to her and gave her hug.

"Dang Majesty you don't miss me?"

"Of course, I do, the two of them were hogging you up."

"Oh, I was about to say, Majesty this is my best bae, Alexis. Alexis this is Majesty my Somalian Hitta." Majesty playfully punched me in my shoulder, she hates when I call her that. We grabbed some lunch at the Somalian fish market. It was so good, I had the fried sword fish stuffed with shrimp and crab meat and pepper and onions and spinach. Alexis ordered a lobster salad typical shit. I'm feeding for two, and this fish is seasoned with the best spices that ever-graced mankind. We finished eating our food. I took my left overs with me. Pure and Eboni's condo wasn't too far from here.

We finally made it to Pure's condo. It was nice and upscale. As soon as you stepped in you could tell that you were in the presence of a queen. It was so immaculate. I loved everything about it. Cathedral ceilings. Her décor was gold and cream. I took a seat on the sofa and kicked my shoes off. Alexis sat right next to me. Pure, Eboni, Majesty sat across from us and grilled the fuck out of us. Of course, Pure spoke up first.

"Journee, what the fuck is going on and why are you here, and where's Kairo?"

"Well for starters Kairo kidnapped me and brought me over here. I want to kill him, and I need your help. The United States Government is after us."

"Hold up Journee are you serious about all of this, are you sure you want to kill Kairo? My loyalty lies with you. Killing someone that you love is hard take it from a woman that knows. Why do you have to kill him?"

"I love Kairo, but I'm not in love with him. It's a lot about him that you don't know. He was still married to his wife the whole time while we were together. I'm back with Juelz. If I don't kill Kairo, he'll come here and do it. I rather he die by my hands than his."

"Journee are you serious? I can't believe that lying motherfucka. I'll kill him for you. Ethiopians are sneaky as fuck. You're finally back with Juelz that's amazing. I told you years ago true love will never die!" Pure was a ball of fire. Eboni and Majesty soaked in everything that I told them.

Alexis grabbed the graph paper and started executing the layout with Majesty. I used Pure's phone to FaceTime Juelz and Alonzo giving them the rundown of our plan they were down. I put Eboni on FaceTime with Juelz, she told Juelz that she has access to the ports in the United States.

Juelz and Alonzo wanted to know if they could ship their guns over using the ports. Eboni said that it was cool he could ship his guns using the same containers that Kairo used to smuggle his diamonds. Pure told Juelz and Alonzo if they wanted to take out Free and Kairo they needed a team because they're considered royalty in Ethiopia. The Hussein Mafia is very powerful throughout South Africa, she suggested that they fly into Somalia instead of Ethiopia because Kairo controls everything moving there.

Majesty said that she had some hittas that would be down to assist with taking out Kairo and Free. Juelz said that he needed to meet them first, he had a team, and he'll be here in about ten days. It takes four days to for the containers to arrive in Somalia. I emailed Juelz the information and the person he needed to see at the port to get started.

I had so much fun with these three today I dread going back to Ethiopia. Majesty and Eboni gave us four guns and some bulletproof vests. We would come back out here in a few days to start training and again when Juelz and Alonzo make it out here. Pure and Eboni took us back to the speed boat and we quickly boarded and headed back to Ethiopia.

***

Two hours later we made back to Ethiopia. We used a local driver at the boat dock to take us back home. I couldn't risk Kairo finding out what I'm up too. We pulled back up at the compound. I put my hand up to the door. Alexis hit the light and Kairo and Free we're sitting in the living room with their guns drawn, that shit didn't scare me.

"Y'all can leave now."

"Where in the fuck have you been?"

"Kairo watch your fucking mouth. I don't know how you to talk to Tyra, but you know better. You can't talk to me like that. The door is that way."

"Kairo you need to handle that shit. I wish Alexis would talk crazy to me like that."

"Fuck you Free you can leave. What the fuck are you going to do? You ain't the only nigga out here strapped." Oh Lord, I could already tell it was about to be some shit and a long night. Alexis had two guns on her. I could tell she was ready to get her hands dirty. I hate being naked without a gun. I went to the kitchen and heated my food up. I wasn't paying Kairo any attention or giving him my energy.

Alexis and Free were still arguing. I ate my food and Kairo was staring a hole in me. If he knew what I knew he would steer, clear of me. I put my food in the trash and walked upstairs to my room and locked the door. I heard the door unlock. I couldn't even undress like I wanted too.

"I asked you a question and you didn't fucking answer me, where were you?"

"Minding my FUCKING BUSINESS! Something you know nothing about."

"Is that my baby you're carrying?"

"Funny you were too busy screwing your wife, you didn't have time to fuck me and satisfy my needs."

"Journee that wasn't the FUCKING case, I told you what it was."

"I don't care Kairo can you leave PLEASE."

"Yeah, but anytime you move around I need to know where the fuck you are at all times. Here is a phone and I'm out."

"You can keep it. I don't need it or anything from you. I need some groceries and your card."

"You still want to spend my money, you can come and stay at our house and eat."

"I refuse too, you can just book me a flight back home and I can turn myself in since I'm wanted."

Chapter-17

Alexis

Free and Kairo we're a trip. Free followed me to my room. I tried to close the door on him, but he pulled my hair and pushed me on the bed.

"Where in the fuck have you been? You can't talk to me how Journee talks to Kairo."

"Free you know I like it rough."

"Oh, you've been giving my pussy up?"

"Bye Free, this pussy doesn't belong to you anymore. You brought your pussy on the plane with you and your daughter. I'm getting this tattoo covered up."

"Alexis, we ain't over until I say we're over." Free took matters into his own hands and started unbuckling my pants trying to fuck. I stopped him right in his tracks.

"Free we're not about to do this. We made our bed now and we're going to lay in it. Don't do what you did to me to Giselle. I'm not cheating on Alonzo, go home to your fiancé."

"Alexis, I was dead ass serious about having my tiger lick on you. I'll kill you for even mentioning another nigga name in my presence."

"I'm not afraid to die, we all have to go some day." If Journee doesn't come in here, right now I swear I will fuck him and send his ass back home to Giselle because he's begging for the pussy. I don't want to cheat on Alonzo but damn I will fuck the shit out of Free, he's tearing my panties off with his teeth. He knows that my weakness.

"Free you have to go. Take your ass home now. Giselle is already coming over here thinking that Alexis wants you, but it's you." Thank God Journee busted up in here when she did. Free walked off and licked his lips. I just shook my head.

"Alexis stop provoking him."

"Journee don't put that shit on me."

"Girl stop! I heard you say Free you know I like it rough."

"Good night Journee thank you." I wanted to fuck Free one last time before I killed him. He always said that my pussy would be the death of him. That was the perfect way to kill him. Fuck him to sleep and blow his brains out. I had an amazing day despite the two pulling up. Majesty, Pure, and Eboni were some cool chicks.

Chapter-18

Giselle

I've been in Ethiopia for about four days. It was cool out here for the most part. I couldn't see myself living out here. I didn't know anybody out here. Free and Kairo were gone most of the day. I stayed at the compound by myself with Kassence.

Tyra was doing her own thing and we haven't spoken at all. It really didn't matter to me anymore because she revealed her true colors weeks ago. I haven't seen Journee and Alexis in about two days either. I've been by there a few times, but they weren't at home. They were up to something. Tonight, Free and Kairo were throwing a party for the Hussein Mafia.

It was an All-White Affair, of course, I was going to shut shit down. I didn't trust any of the women that worked here, they were always looking at me and laughing. I caught the way they looked at Free. I found a seamstress to make me a dress. She did and amazing job the color was perfect, and it fit me like a glove. I was snatched my body sat up perfect.

Free's grandparents were watching Kassence for me. Maybe tonight I can meet an African Prince. I sat in the mirror and beat my face. I was going for a nude look. I heard the door crack I didn't pay it any mind.

"Aye sexy you look good tonight." I ignored Free and rolled my eyes and kept right on doing my makeup. Free has been acting real funny since we came here. We barely spend any time together. I know he's cheating or doing something. Since I've been here I've learned to pray and don't worry about anything that I can't control. I'm tired of running up behind niggas that don't want me. I'm ready to turn a new leaf. If it's not about my daughter, it's not about nothing. Free broke me out of my thoughts and started sucking on my neck.

"Can you please stop. Go suck on whoever you've been sucking on."

"Giselle, it ain't nobody but you. You know I'm out here grinding. I brought you a brand-new Porsche truck. I didn't hear you complaining about that.

"Free you've been grinding since I've met you, but since we've been out here you've changed. You've always had time for me and your daughter, but now we don't have any time. I'm ready to go back home."

"This is home. You're living in a mansion. You have staff that works for you. You have access to all my money. What more do you want, are you ready to get married?" Free still didn't get it.

I just ignored him and finished my makeup. He knelt in front of me and tried to raise my dress up past my thighs.

"Stop I'm trying to get dressed."

"I can't eat my pussy before we leave?"

"No Free, because we'll end up fucking and not going anywhere. I really want to go to this party." I wasn't fucking him or letting him suck on me. I know he's fucking somebody. Whoever this bitch was she wore White Diamond perfume and she wore too much of it. I went through Free's clothes and they all had the same scent. Whoever she was she was leaving her mark. Free thought I was dumb but I'm hip. Normally I would've been down for some get back shit just to have one up on him, but I'm good on that. The next nigga I fuck will be my husband. Free didn't ease up he ate my pussy like he wanted too. I rode the shit out of his face, but it wasn't going to be any fucking.

***

Two hours later and we were completely dressed and ready to go to the party. This party was the talk of the country. Free hired us a driver to drive us. He held my hand in the back seat. Ugh, I knew Free was a dog, but it was really starting to show now.

"I love you Giselle never question that."

"Actions speak louder than words." Free wanted to reassure me. I had a good feeling about tonight, but my eye kept twitching. I knew something was about to happen. I said a quick prayer and prayed for the best. We finally made it to the party. All eyes were on us like I knew they would. Damn these were some handsome African men I've always had a wondering eye. The African women just stared and turned their noses up. Damn, they act like their skin is the only one that has Melanin I'm black and just as beautiful. My skin is popping too like never before. Journee gave me some pure coconut butter to keep my skin moisturized, oh my god my skin glistened before I go back home I'm taking this shit home by the cases.

A few women stopped me and asked me about my hair. I could do hair really good, I might go to school to get my hair license and open a salon. I cut my hair into a symmetrical bob. I flat ironed it bone straight it draped right over my shoulders. I walked with confidence in the party and held my head up high. Free kept holding my hand as we moved through the party. The African music was nice, they treated us like Royalty we sipped champagne out of gold wine glasses with diamonds on the rim.

The party was really nice everything was white and gold. Big chandeliers with crystals and diamonds. Gold statues of kings and queens. It was luxurious real tigers at the entrance.

A lot of the men that Free introduced me too, their wives were friendly and complemented and I complemented them also. I looked around the room to see if I saw Journee or Alexis, but I didn't see them, this party was filled to capacity.

Kairo and Tyra approached us with a few other people. I noticed this one chick she kept looking at me funny. She looked me up and down. She tapped me and extended her hand for me to shake it, something told me not too. She rubbed me the wrong way. I smelled the loud White Diamond perfume on her. Tyra smiled at me. I grilled the fuck out of this bitch. I can't believe I was even cool with her snake ass. I swear she's a fake bitch. Plastic surgery couldn't even fix Journee's name on her face.

"I don't shake hands." I could never smile up in a bitch face and openly fuck her man. If I didn't know you then I don't owe you any loyalty. It's fuck you and you would say the same about me.

"Do you think that you're better than me or something? I watched you shake everybody's hand but mine." She had the thickest African accent I ever heard of. I had to look with my stank face.

"Are you talking to me?" I had to ask this bitch because I was ready to check her and Tyra.

"Who else would I be talking too?"

"I don't know you, but I'm sure you've heard all about me from Tyra. I'm Giselle the mother of Free's daughter and his fiancé. I would never shake a bitches hand that's fucking my fiancé. I'm low but not that low. Your old ass perfume gave you up THIRSTY." The party got quiet and all the attention and eyes were on us. Tyra whispered to her friends in their language. I looked at Free with so much disgust. This bitch isn't even cute the only thing she had was some big ass titties and a big African ass that's it.

Free looked at me begging me not to cut up. He's not even worth it. I guess the saying is true how you gain a nigga is the same way you lose him. I turned my back to walk away I needed a stiff drink. I'm not even a drinker but I needed something to calm me down because my eye was still twitching. As soon as I took a few steps and approached the bar, someone ran up behind me and hit me in the head with a statue.

I instantly had a reflex and I was quick on my toes. I spun around so quick and started fighting the girl that was with Tyra. This would be the first fight that I won. I'm tired of losing. I picked up the statue and smashed it in her face, blood was leaking everywhere, and it splattered on my dress I didn't care. I had on my Red bottoms, I stepped out of them, so I wouldn't lose my balance.

I was getting the best of her. All of a sudden, Tyra and three other girls were jumping me. I was shoved down to the grown. I got in a fetal position trying to protect my faces punches were coming from everywhere. Free and Kairo didn't even break it up.

This older lady with long beautiful locs, she started getting them off me, and laying them out. I'm forever grateful that she got them off me. My body was sore, they pulled my hair out. I had a few gashes on my head. Blood was everywhere. My dress was ruined. I was so embarrassed. I looked for Free and he was cleaning this bitches wounds.

"My child I'm sorry those skunks teamed up on you. I know you're not from here I couldn't stand around and let them beat you not in front of my eyes."

"Thank you, I appreciate it. I'm grateful for you helping me and getting them off me."

"You welcome anytime. Who are you with?"

"Kasson(Free) Hussein."

"Oh, do you know my daughter Journee Leigh, she used to date Kairo's sleazy ass?"

"Yes, mam I do know her."

"Good I'll take you to her compound, so I can clean your wounds and nurse you back to good health. Call me momma Edith."

"Thank you, momma Edith." Momma Edith saved my life. They did me so dirty. I just knew that I wouldn't live to see another day. Free should've never let that happen. Five women jumped little ole me and Free and Kairo didn't do a damn thing. He's a fucking coward. I need to get my daughter, I don't have anywhere to go. I wonder if I could stay with Journee until we all figured how to get back home. Real bitches do real things. Never in a million years, I would've thought that Tyra would do me like that. I rode with her right or wrong.

***

We made it to Journee's compound about twenty minutes later. Momma Edith stopped by a pharmacy and got some bandages. I was unconscious my body hurt. I wanted to cry so bad I couldn't even look in the mirror. I know I looked bad. I noticed how everybody looked at me when she carried me out. It was a little after 1:00 am, I had a hard time getting out of the car. She picked me up and put me on her back and made her way toward the door.

Momma Edith knocked on Journee's door like a mad woman. I didn't need the dirty looks from Alexis. Journee seems like she has a lot of compassion. The door swung open and it was Alexis. Momma Edith moved Alexis out of the way and laid me on the sofa. Alexis was the last person that I wanted to see. She looked at me and tears filled the brim of her eyes.

"Hi Momma Edith, Giselle who did this to you, oh my God let me go wake up Journee."

"Fill the tub up Alexis with warm water so I can clean her up."

"Ok momma." Alexis ran through the compound to wake Journee up. Journee trotted down the stairs, she came in the living room, she wiped the sleep out of her eyes.

"Momma Edith is that you? Giselle come here what the fuck happened to you."

"Tyra and four girls jumped me at Free's party."

"Where were Free and Kairo?"

"They were there they just stood and watched. Free was messing with one of the girls and she got mad at me because I refused to shake her hand."

"Alexis let's go! It took all of them to jump you, and these niggas didn't do shit? It ain't that type of motherfucking party. I'm a kill a bitch tonight a few of them."

"No Journee you don't have to do anything. Juelz would kill me if something happened to you and his child. I'll handle them. I don't have anywhere to go, can my daughter and I stay here with you until I figure out how to get us back home, please? I refuse to go back to that house."

"Alexis is it ok with you? I don't want to make you uncomfortable?"

"I'm fine with it, I wouldn't have it any other way. That's fucked up, Tyra and her friends need to die a slow death. I owe that bitch one anyway. I don't wish bad on nobody." I'm grateful that Journee and Alexis took me in despite our past. They were ready to ride for me and. I'm not a part of their circle it was genuine. If it wasn't for the real, you wouldn't recognize the fake. I'm so thankful.

Momma Edith sat me in the bath tub and washed me up with warm water. She brushed the knots out of my hair. She went outside and got me a few Aloe Vera leaves and spread the pure Shea butter in between the leaves and rubbed it on my wounds. The hot bath was relaxing. Journee gave me a room with some fresh pajamas and a cup of hot tea and some coffee cake. I felt a lot better being here I could sleep and not think about if the workers we're going to hurt me.

Journee, Alexis, and Momma Edith went to get Kassence for me and my things. I didn't want my daughter around those crazy people. I could never look at Free the same anymore. It upsets me just thinking about it. Tyra, she was my daughters Godmother how could she do that to me? I cried myself to sleep.

Chapter-19

Momma Edith

The Lord doesn't make any mistakes. It was a reason that I went to the party. It was like Giselle was a child of mine. I couldn't stand by and let them do her like that it was so wrong. I don't care how much power the Hussein Mafia and Tyra have. Anybody can be touched, and they're not excluded.

"Journee and Alexis, am I missing something? What was the reason that you had to ask Alexis was it ok for her to stay? She came with you guys what was the problem?" Journee and Alexis gave me the rundown of what happened between the three of them. I soaked in everything that they told me. I had to be careful with my choice of words. The problem with this generation today they take everything for granted and ignore signs. I needed them to understand where I was coming from and why I'm doing what I'm doing.

"You two listen to what I'm about to tell you, and take heed to what I'm saying."

"YES, momma."

"I've seen plenty of women get jumped and I've never interfered. It was something about her spirit that I was drawn too and telling me to help her. I don't know what it is, but it's something. She has been through a lot; her eyes are the keys to her soul. I'm not the one to pry because you two have said enough. She's a day away from losing it. I know y'all past wasn't peachy but as far as y'all future that's different. God puts people in your life for a reason and a season.

Loyalty is priceless. Giselle didn't owe you any loyalty as far as the past. Juelz and Free did. Journee, you need to let that shit go and you do too Alexis. Kairo and Free don't mean y'all ANY good. I told you that years ago Journee to leave him alone, but you didn't listen.

I watched the two of them let that girl get her ass handed to her. My CHILD she needs help. Don't block your blessing by not being there for her. If it's too much on you two she can stay at my house. She's been mistreated enough. When I met you Journee I didn't know you from a can of paint, but it was something about your spirit that drawn me to you.

God told me to help Giselle she's my child too. All I'm saying is put your differences aside and team up, so you can take your ass home. She needs to be around real people. I don't know what y'all planning, but take her with y'all, so she can train with the girls. She needs strength and motivation and guidance be that for her."

"Can you, do it?"

"Yes, momma."

"Good, let's go get her daughter and clothes."

Journee

I understood everything that Momma Edith was saying. I let that little bullshit go years ago. I said what I had to say when she came to my house with Tyra. Yeah, I smacked the fuck out of her on the plane, but I was just being messy because I was upset. What more could I do to Giselle?

She couldn't beat me. I already had Juelz in the bag I'm selfish when it comes to loving him. He broke my heart I vowed to keep his forever. It's not a bitch breathing that could take him from me. I felt so bad for Giselle that was so wrong of them.

I've never ganged anybody, that could've very well been me and Alexis tonight, but something told me don't go to that party. I swear I would've killed every person in that party. I couldn't believe Kairo and Free, how could you do the mother of your child like that. Alexis and Momma Edith went inside Kairo and Free's grand-parent's house to grab Kassence.

Next stop was to Free's compound to get her clothes. I swear the Lord better have me a seat right next to my mother and father all of this charity work that I'm doing. Kassence hugged me so tight she wouldn't let me go. I swear this was the sweetest little girl she's so precious.

We made it back to my compound with all of Giselle and Kassence's stuff. Giselle was sleeping peacefully. We didn't wake her. Momma Edith unpacked all of Giselle's things for her and placed them neatly in the drawers.

If Momma Edith fucked with you than it had to mean something had to be genuine about you. Kassence asked could she sleep with me? I didn't mind. I had to FaceTime Juelz. I put Kassence to bed and she was knocked out quick. I hit the FaceTime app on the laptop and he answered.

"Hey, you sleep?"

"I was laying down what's up?"

"I was just thinking about you before I went to sleep, and I wanted to tell you what happened."

"What happened are you ok, is my son good?"

"I'm fine Juelz we don't even know if it's a boy yet, and you're going to wake Kassence up."

"What is she doing over there?" I gave Juelz the rundown of what happened, he was pissed.

"Journee let me keep it real with you. I appreciate you for looking out because you don't have too. I loved Giselle, but I was never in love with her. You always had my heart.

No matter what I don't want to see her doing bad and fucked off. I'll be out there in about a week to bring you home." I felt a whole lot better about the situation after talking to him.

Chapter-20

Juelz

The guns have been shipped and Eboni and Journee hit me up and told me everything has arrived. Journee thinks that I'm flying out next week. My flight leaves tomorrow. Eboni and Pure hooked me up with a house out in Somalia to rent for two weeks.

I had Alonzo and Skeet with me. Khadir was on board. Alonzo brought three of his partners Dro, Skill, Chaos. I left Smoke behind to watch after Nikki, God Momma Valerie, and Khadijah. Journee didn't know but once she touched down in Somalia. I had no plans for her returning back to Ethiopia.

I refuse to lay without her another night. My daughter wanted to come out here with me to get her mother, but I couldn't risk my baby girl out here because her daddy was about to get dirty out here in the jungle fucking with these fuck niggas. I could easily go back to the states after Journee comes to Somalia, but I had to kill that nigga. He tried me, more than once so he has to learn the hard way.

I had all of my stuff packed. I dropped Jueleez off at my mother's house. Jueleez hugged me so tight, she didn't want me to leave. I had to bring her mother home, that was my only agenda. I had my attorney looking into Journee's case it was bogus, but she still had to turn herself in. I headed over Skeet's house, Khadir was already there.

Alonzo was going to meet us at a private airway strip. My old connect gave it to me years ago. I never used it before. I just kept everything up and running properly and serviced.

***

It was a little after 6:00 am our flight is scheduled to leave at 8:00 am. Journee wanted to talk all night. I couldn't because I had an early flight and I would see her in a few days. The hard part about the flight it's twenty-four hours. Journee calls me every night and I wouldn't be able to answer for two days. I told Nikki don't tell her shit. I wanted to surprise her.

We're doing a layover in Dubai. My cousin Rick is stationed over there he's on vacation and he's going to assist me with taking out Kairo and Free. My connect let me use his pilot to fly us over there. I hope it wasn't any strings attached because I was through with that lifestyle. I dodged penitentiary chances so many times. I had to bow out gracefully. I was running my mother crazy. I have more money than I know what to do with.

Journee and I have been discussing opening a few businesses. I wanted to do real estate. I have the money to buy the properties. I want to learn the back end of the business as far as building permits. I'll let Journee handle the front end.

Journee had her real estate license, she said that she'll go to the class with me she wanted some additional certifications.

Chapter-21

Giselle

I've been at Journee's house for a week. I'm finally gaining my strength back. Momma Edith has been here every step of the way looking out for me and Kassence. My scars have finally healed. The patches of my hair that were pulled out have finally started to fill back in. Momma Edith made me a hair regimen to grow my hair back.

Alexis and Journee have been really nice to me the entire time. I didn't feel like the outcast. I've been traveling back and forth with them to Somalia. I met Pure, Eboni and Majesty. We were training for something they never told me for what.

I started exercising along with them. I learned how to shoot a gun properly and kick box. I couldn't thank them enough. They didn't leave me out of anything that they've done the past week. Kassence loved the both of them, she slept with Journee every night. I was a little jealous behind that.

Apart of me still feels bad about all the bull shit that I did to the both of them. It's funny because they're all I have out here. I don't know how I would ever repay them. Free came by here the other day I opened the door and he turned right back around. Kassence was yelling at him and he ignored her.

I wanted to talk with Momma Edith because I trust her like she's my mother on what should I do. She was out in the garden relaxing. I just want to right my wrongs. I went outside to join her.

"Momma can I talk to you for a minute."

"Sure, my child what's bothering you?"

"I want to right my wrongs. I can't get over the fact that I did Journee and Alexis wrong and they're here helping me hen Free and Tyra isn't. I can't get over it. It won't leave my mind and get out of my head."

"Have you asked for their forgiveness? They need to apologize also."

"No, I haven't done that."

"That's your first step. Apologize and they need to do the same. Two wrongs don't make a right." I took Momma Edith's advice and marched in the house. We weren't going to Somalia today because Journee and Alexis didn't feel good. I knew Journee was pregnant, but Alexis was tight lipped about her shit. Everybody was laying around in the living room lounging.

"Can I talk to the two of you for a minute?"

"Sure."

"Let me start with you, Alexis. I'm sorry for continuing to pursue Free while openly knowing that you two had something going on. Can you forgive me? I really appreciate you for helping me, when I didn't have anyone. It means so much to me. I was young and dumb, but I'm growing."

"I forgive you Giselle, it's something that I would like to forget. I'm sorry for putting my hands on you when I should've just killed Free with all of the anger that I built up."

"Journee I'm sorry. I had no business coming to your house about Juelz and I apologize. I just couldn't believe that he left me for you. I didn't want to accept that. The love that he has for you nobody can come between that, it was very selfish of me because eight years later and nothing has changed you still have him. I'm sorry can you forgive me? I can't tell you enough how much I appreciate you for taking me and my daughter in."

"Girl you're good! I'm not tripping off that shit, that was the past."

"Journee don't you think that you need to apologize too?"

"Yes, momma I was I have manners I was getting there. I'm sorry Giselle for putting my hands on you and it is taking it there. My mother is everything to me and when you said something about her it was a wrap. You have a smart-ass mouth. I'm sorry for putting my hands on you in front of Kassence." It felt good to get the extra weight and burdens off my chest. We sat around and talked and kicked it for a few.

Journee and Alexis wanted to go in town to the local shops. I've never been there before. Momma Edith was watching

Kassence and we were taking her car. Journee and Alexis told me to dress down. I don't have any tennis shoes or shorts. I only brought dresses and skirts. Journee gave me a cute jogging suit that hasn't been worn yet and some Fenty Pumas to put on.

"Why do I need to dress down?"

"You never know Giselle, you have to be prepared at all times. We might run into Tyra and her friends, and we might have to beat some ass."

"Ok Alexis."

"Do you have your gun on you?"

"Yes Journee."

"Good let's roll." I guess they told me they were always prepared to beat some ass. I like that about them if I wasn't the victim. I wanted to get Tyra and her friends. After training with Journee and her crew. I knew they couldn't fuck with me if I was to see them again.

Alexis

I felt bad for Giselle. I don't know if it's the pregnancy hormones or what, but they did her dirty. I always knew that Tyra wasn't shit from the moment I laid eyes on her. I was so glad when Kairo met Journee. I know she genuinely cared about him and she wasn't with him for his money. To actually think I wanted to fuck Free one last time.

How could you do that to the mother of your child? He was pissed that I touched her, but you let five females jump her and not break that shit up. My mind was really blown after that, he had the nerve to come by here like shit was cool. Journee and I saw him through the window and we made sure Giselle opened the door and he turned around. No nigga you can't even come in my presence the next time you'll see me is when I kill you.

Journee and I wanted to go back to that party so bad and body every one of them bitches. It's all good though we'll see them real soon. Giselle was a natural she could shoot really good. When the time presents itself, I hope she's ready to bust, we ain't take her with us for nothing.

Everybody was quiet on the ride to the local shops. I was thinking about Alonzo something serious. I couldn't wait to see him. I haven't told him about the baby yet. I wanted to FaceTime him, but Journee hogs up the laptop every night with Juelz. I'm sure once we get back home, I won't be able to see much of her and she won't to see much of me either.

"Damn y'all are quiet, what's up?"

"Ugh, are you sure you want to know Alexis? I'm thinking about how you slammed me into the car. I would've never thought you were that strong. I almost passed out when you shot Free."

"I wasn't even going to fight you Giselle, but you provoked me. Your mouth is too fucking smart and you kept coming for me. I had to get at you."

"I'm sorry, but y'all know y'all was rude as fuck especially you Journee. The moment you came to the door, I knew your sister looked familiar. I knew shit was about to go left. We shouldn't have come to your house, but I was riding with my friend at that time. Journee, she knew Kairo didn't want her, she was blackmailing him. He really divorced her, the day we came to your house. She called me after she got served, he tricked her into signing some papers.

I should've known then that she was fraud, she would always tell me to leave Juelz and be with Free, but she would never leave Kairo knowing damn well he didn't want her ass." Giselle wasn't that bad once you got to know her.

She was pretty cool chick a little bougie, but she was all right. She was starting to grow on me. Kassence was so adorable. I wanted a boy I don't even know if Alonzo wants a kid we never used protection. I have too many girls Nyla and Jueleez are enough. I can't wait to wrap with Nikki and Khadijah when I get back. I miss them so much.

Chapter-22

Journee

I needed some fresh air. I was tired this baby was draining me and taking all of my energy. I need some sleep bad. I decided not to go to Somalia today. I wanted some soul food. Fried chicken, pinto beans, baked mac n cheese, and buttermilk cornbread. I promised Kassence that I would make her some banana pudding, that was why we had to come to the local market to get everything that I needed to cook. The market was about twenty minutes from my compound.

We pulled up at the market. It was extremely busy as always. I parked the car up front. We made our way inside of the store. Alexis grabbed the cart and Giselle had the list to make sure that we didn't forget anything we needed. We headed over to the meat department first to get a whole chicken. The Ethiopians seasoned the chicken really good with a red spice and herb it was amazing. I grabbed some peanut oil also.

We had to get some snacks for Kassence. The chocolate was so rich here with no artificial flavoring I loved it. The soda tasted so much better, that's one of the reasons I loved it here so much. Everything was organic. Giselle wanted some ice cream, so we went to that department last it was near the registers.

"How could y'all hang with someone that fucked the both of your men?" I knew that wasn't Tyra. I had to turn around and look just to make sure that it wasn't her and it was. I nudged Giselle and she nudged Alexis. I ignored her, trust me she didn't want any noise.

"Tyra is that the same female who I beat up at the party last week? I grabbed Giselle because she was about to turn around and say something.

"Not here, I whispered. Alexis already knew what time it was. They kept talking shit.

"Journee and Alexis the two of you are some of the dumbest hoes I ever ran across to kick it with Giselle. She fucked Juelz and Free." I had to turn around and say something.

"Tyra, I didn't want to have to school you, but you're begging for too much attention. Real women do real things. I don't give a fuck who Giselle fucked. Real women empower each other and uplift each other." Tyra was still talking shit, her, and the other girl. If she was dumb enough to follow us out here to this car. Today she would take her last breath and I put that on my momma.

She followed us to check out still talking shit. I had to beg Giselle and Alexis not to cut the fuck up in this store. Damn I hope Tyra ain't this fucking dumb, she saw first-hand how I came at my house, being in Ethiopia would be no different.

Well, Tyra was just as dumb as I thought she was. She wanted to pick a fight so bad in front of her friend. I wasn't about to give her that and go to jail for killing her in broad daylight. We loaded the groceries into the car.

I pulled out and Tyra and two other cars were right behind me. It was a little river called the little Blue Nile not too far from here. If she follows me I'm disposing of her fucking body, being with Kairo he's taught me how to do a lot of shit.

"Giselle get ready to catch your first body."

"What's that mean Journee?"

"Are you going to get your ass beat or protect yourself?"

"Protect me."

"Ok because your friend is still following us. I'm about to pull over by this river and if this bitch and her friends get out. I'm killing them all. Alexis get the gloves out of my purse. Giselle make sure gun is locked and fucking loaded it only about five minutes to kill a bitch. Follow my lead."

"Journee let's do this shit. Giselle if you're scared keep your ass in the fucking car."

"Alexis I'm more than fucking ready. They tried my whole life and fucked up my appearance. Let me put my Vaseline on first."

"Girl come on you don't need no Vaseline." Everybody was on the same page. We made it to the river. Everybody's gun was tucked behind their waist locked and loaded and ready to go. We played it off cool as we approached the river.

We were laughing and talking shit. I'm sick of this bitch I owe her one anyway. It has nothing to do with Kairo, she's been disrespectful since I've met her. The moment she shot the van up it was on from there. I couldn't stand a weak ass bitch. We posted up by these big ass rocks near the nape of the river. No one was over here because this end of the river is shallow. I'm just waiting to see how this is about to play out.

"I finally caught you off guard Journee. Let's fight bitch. I wish you would do me how you did me at your house." Tyra was crazy as hell. I wasn't about to fight this bitch. I was shooting her stupid ass. Fuck that she needs her ass whooped again. I knew I shouldn't be fighting because I'm pregnant, but this bitch was asking for it.

I could've sworn I did this hoe dirty a few weeks ago at my house. She wanted to show out in front of her friends okay. She approached me and attempted to swing at me. I let her get that one swing in. I grabbed her fist and punched her in the eye with her own fist dummy.

I gave that hoe some fresh work. I had so much anger built up, and she was about to get all of it. I slammed her into the rocks her head was fucking leaking. I wasn't finished yet. I needed some more blood on my hands. She stumbled a little bit. I kicked her in her stomach, she fell back. I stood over her. I shot that bitch right in between her eyes, close range stupid bitch.

"Giselle, we're going to do two things before we end these bitches. I want you to go toe to toe with all four of them. The first bitch that thinks she wants to jump in, depending on how I'm feeling. I'm going to shoot that bitch in the back of her head.

Alexis, if you want to jump in so they can see how it feels to get jumped. Do your thing. Which one of y'all African hoes got next?" Her friends started to back the fuck up. Giselle wasn't playing with these hoes today. She was passing out straight work. Face shots and body blows. I saw her kick box a few bitches too. She had so much energy and anger built up.

It was crazy I didn't think she had it in her. She stomped one chick out so bad, her eye popped out of its pupil my heart jumped. Alexis and Giselle start knocking those bitches back one by one. Three down and two to go. One tried to run, and I shot that bitch in the back of her head. Alexis shot the other one.

No face no case. Training with Somalian Hittas they made sure that every gun we had come with the red beam. They trained us to shoot straight head shots nothing more nothing less.

We dragged the bodies to the middle of the river and watched them sink. I collected the gloves and made sure and sprayed salt water on our skin, so no DNA would be traceable. I would burn the gloves when we get back to the compound.

"Giselle, you good?"

"I'm great." We walked back to the car like nothing happened. This was my first kill. I kept having flashbacks but I'm sure the Lord would forgive me for my sins. I was protecting myself. Nobody spoke a word. It's killed or be killed. I'm hungry too and ready to fry my chicken.

Juelz

We finally made it to Somalia, we stayed in Dubai for a day to kick it with my cousin Ricky. He brought two of his partners with him. My eyes landed across some bad bitches in Dubai, but Journee was the only one that had my eye.

Eboni, Majesty, and Pure picked us up from the airport. I know I just got here, but I'm an impatient ass nigga. I know I planned to stay in Somalia for a week, but fuck that. I'm ready to head to Ethiopia right now and get this bullshit over with. Skeet and Alonzo already knew what time it was. I wanted Kairo to feel me.

Journee didn't know that Kairo was coming when he kidnapped her, but that motherfucka was going to know that I was coming. Alonzo's cousin Asia worked for the FEDS she bagged Efren and had him to come down to the morgue to claim Kairo's mother's body. Asia took a picture of that shit and sent me a copy in HD. It takes two hours to get to Ethiopia from Somalia.

I traced Kairo's cell phone number down from when Journee FaceTime Jueleez from his phone. I knew his every move. I love to play chess, but I'm ready to checkmate this motherfucka. I rep Zoo Atlanta until the death of me. I'll go ape shit anywhere.

"Pure, I'm ready to do this shit tonight."

"Juelz are you sure?"

"I'm more than sure."

"Ok we can take some boats to Ethiopia, but you have to wear a disguise as some local Ethiopians. Y'all stick out like a sore thumb."

"I'm ready to do this shit and get it over with. What do I have to do?"

"It's still early if we leave now, the sun will still be up when we get there. I would have to find some clothes for all of you and a few camels for you to ride on."

"Camels, street niggas don't ride camels Pure."

"Look Juelz you're in Africa and niggas in Ethiopia don't dress like you or look like you. We can't hop off a boat in Ethiopia looking like a trap star or rapper you have to blend in. If you're trying to leave now you're going to need some local attire to cover your face and you to ride on a camel. If we wait until later when night falls none of that shit will be necessary."

"It is what is I'm ready to go. Pure and Eboni shook their head at me and laughed. I didn't give a fuck. Kairo and I can shoot it out in broad daylight, wherever however fuck a disguise. I just wanted Journee and my son home.

She's been gone for too long. I refuse to look my daughter in the face another day and her mother isn't home. It's all good I'm a man of my word. Journee is coming home today. I'm ready to slang this AK like a guitar.

Journee

I'm really getting irritated now and I've been calling Juelz for the past two days and he hasn't answered. I called Nikki to see if Skeet had heard from him or knew where he was. She was acting all nonchalant, talking about I haven't called her in two weeks. Why would I call her today, because I'm pregnant and I'm looking for my baby daddy?

I needed to hear his voice. I miss the fuck out of him. I'm ready to go home.

"Journee, you have company."

"I'm not expecting anyone Giselle." She gave me a faint smile. Kairo pushed passed her and made his way into my room and slammed the door.

"Look Kairo you can leave with all of that bullshit."

"Journee did you fucking kill her?"

"What do you think? When that bitch shot up the van, and you didn't do or say shit to her about it you knew I was going to get at her. I should've killed that bitch weeks ago. Everything that she got she deserved that shit. If you loved her that much you should've kept that bitch away from me."

"Come with me now!"

"No, I'm not going with you."

"You don't have a fucking choice."

"I do just leave."

"If you don't bring your ass on now, I'm cutting the power off over here and you will be forced to stay with me. You won't be able to talk to Juelz every night. Yeah, I know all about that shit." I put my shoes on and followed behind him. Giselle and Kassence looked at me as I followed him out the door.

Alexis looked at me and I grilled the fuck out of her. I was pissed she knew what that meant. I got in the car with Kairo and slammed the door as hard as I could. I couldn't stand him after he watched Giselle get beat up by five women it was really a wrap.

"Don't slam my fucking door like you crazy Journee." I ignored him. He grabbed my hand and I snatched it away from him. He pulled the car over on the side of the road. He put the car in park and hopped out and opened the passenger door.

"Get the fuck out Journee. I'm tired of you trying my fucking hand." I got out of the car and placed my arms on my chest and grilled him.

"What Kairo?" He just looked at me and paced back and forth like he was crazy. I don't have time for this shit. I got ready to walk back toward my compound and he ran up on me.

"Journee, why did you have to kill her?"

"Kairo, ask the bitch when you see her again why did she provoke me and follow me."

Chapter-23

Kairo

Man, I couldn't believe Journee killed Tyra. It was cameras inside of the market. Tyra was on camera fucking with the three of them. Her father called me and said that she hasn't come since earlier and he tried calling her cellphone and she didn't answer.

Her father knew that she went to the marker earlier. I went up to the market to see if my partner Sampson or has anybody seen her. He showed me the video tape of her fucking with Journee and Giselle. I put two and two together, I knew Journee had to do something with her disappearing, but I didn't know what.

Where were the fucking bodies and her car? So, I can dispose of that shit properly.

"Journee, where's the body?"

"Little Blue Nile River."

"You dumped her body?"

"Yes." Damn Journee wasn't bullshitting. I drove to Little Blue Nile River it was about forty-five minutes from here. I had to make sure that it wasn't any evidence of Journee at the crime scene. I sent a message to Free I needed him to help me dispose of her car.

"Where are your gloves?"

"I disposed of them."

"Did anybody see you?"

"No."

"Why didn't you call me?"

"Why would I call you Kairo? I don't even know who you are anymore. Giselle told us what happened to her at the party. I couldn't believe you would do that shit. I would expect that from Free but not you."

"Let me explain."

"Save it." I've come to terms that Journee and I will never be, too much shit has happened and she's hard headed as fuck and she doesn't want to listen, but I'm ok with that. Tyra had to go anyway. Mia told me that she was a witness in my case. I didn't want Journee to do it because she's never killed anybody before. I trained her to kill if she was ever in a fucked-up situation she could handle hers.

She seems to be ok. Free finally pulled with Shyheim and Manu. I couldn't call the clean-up crew because some of them worked for Tyra and her family. It'll be a war if her family found out that Journee killed her. They wanted Journee dead anyway, but I wasn't about to let shit happen to her.

Free came to the car and tapped the window. I hopped out. Journee stayed in the car. We doused each car with gasoline. I grabbed Tyra's purse and phone out of her car.

We sat back and watched each vehicle burn to the ground. Free had a chemical to put out the fire. I had a pick-up truck coming to pick up the remain articles of the car. I didn't need anything leading back to me.

***

Two hours later everything was cleaned up. Free drove the pickup truck. Shyheim and Manu drove his car. They had to kill the driver of the pick-up truck. I don't trust anybody a motherfucka will sale they soul for the right price. Journee and I drove in silence back to her compound.

She didn't say shit to me and I didn't say shit to her. She could go home in a few weeks. Tyra was working with the FEDS with her dead and her brother dead also they didn't have a case or any witnesses to testify. I might go back to the states, but I doubt it. The FEDS still wanted me because they heard about me.

I pulled back up to Journee's compound she was about to open the door and get out. I grabbed her shirt, she turned around and looked at me.

"You can go home in a few weeks. Tyra was working with the FEDS. She and her brother are both dead."

"Okay." She continued to get out of the car. I grabbed her shirt again. She looked at me and gave me the meanest scowl ever.

"No matter what you think, and how you may feel about me. I loved you and I wanted you to be my wife. The life we shared together was real. It was never about her, it was always about you. No matter who I'm with and when I die everything that I have will go to you. You were the realest female that I met, and you wanted me for me and not what I could do for you."

"Good-bye Kairo." I put myself out there. I wanted Journee to know how I feel. She irritated the fuck out of me. She's holding a grudge against me. With time heals all wounds. My phone alerted me that I had a text message. I couldn't check my messages right now because Journee's compound was a mile away from mine, and the road was so dark and narrow. No street lights and I didn't want to swerve and hit something.

I don't even know why I got her, her own compound here. Whatever I had she had. It's crazy we were throwing eight years away behind a mistake. I fucked up I didn't see it then, but I see it now. I should've left Tyra when I said I did and we wouldn't be here.

I felt our relationship was salvageable. Journee is one female that can't be bought. I wish shit would've played out different, but it didn't.

I finally made it to my house. I got my stuff out of the car. I looked at my phone because it beeped again. I grabbed my phone out of my pocket. I had a picture message from and unknown number. I opened the picture and it was a picture of my mother dead and my cousin Efren.

My body shook Who would kill my mother? The message read.

Unknown- You took what belongs to me, so I killed this bitch

Oh, so this was Juelz. Let me call Free, he answered on the first ring.

"Yo."

"Aye Free meet me at Journee's house. Juelz killed momma."

"What the fuck you say Kairo?"

"You heard me. I don't want to repeat this shit." It's not a bitch alive that can take my mother's place.

"Journee better put that pussy ass nigga on the right now, when I get over there." If he killed my momma I am leaving this bitch tonight and I'm at his doorstep in the morning. I sped to Journee's house and threw my car into park. I kicked her fucking door open and off the hinges. I don't give a fuck.

"Kairo don't bust up in her like this."

"Alexis shut the fuck up talking to me and get the fuck out my way. I don't hit women, but I will smack the fuck out of you right now." I pushed passed Alexis and ran up the stairs to Journee's room. I slammed the door she was in the shower. I yanked the curtains back and she looked at me and turned her head.

"Get the fuck out right now! She closed the curtain. I snatched the curtain back and stepped into the shower and picked her up and threw her over my shoulder and tossed her on her bed.

"I'm going to kill Juelz that pussy motherfucka killed my momma. Get his ass on the fucking phone now."

"You call him."

"I'm tired of you playing with me. Do what the fuck I say do Journee. I'm not in my right state of mind. I will fucking kill you because you mean a lot to him, but if he killed my mother. I will take you away from him and not give a fuck. Body for a body." She wanted to cry save those fucking tears.

"I don't have anything to do with that."

"Yes, the fuck you do. I'm going to fuck you first and record it, so he can see it and then I'm going to kill you." I'm dead ass serious. Fuck Journee this nigga killed my fucking mom she's the air I breathe all bets where fucking off.

"What's his fucking number?"

"I don't know."

"Give it to me Journee! I want him to watch me fuck you and kill you sense he thinks this shit is a fucking game. You should've told him about me."

"Move Kairo leave. Stop dragging me into your mess." Journee wasn't saying shit that I wanted to hear. I grabbed her laptop and hit the FaceTime button. I wanted Juelz to see my balls deep in my pussy one last time because this was the last time that he would see Journee with my dick dug deep into her.

He crossed the fucking line, my line. If he was bold enough to touch my mother I'm wiping his whole blood line out behind my mother. I will due time in the FEDS behind my momma and escape like El Chapo. Journee's laptop connected.

"Open your fucking legs and give me this pussy." She wanted to fight me.

"Journee, I don't mind taking your pussy." I pushed her legs open, so he could see. I grabbed my gun from behind my waist, pulled the trigger back and pointed to her head.

"Please don't do this."

"A bitch gone die today YOU."

Chapter -24

Juelz

Kairo got my picture message. I had Journee's compound surrounded and he didn't even know it. I watched him when he pulled off and pulled back up. Eboni called her mother, who was already at Journee's compound and told her to let us in when they were gone.

We've been in the basement the whole time. I heard that fuck nigga talking all of that shit. I was waiting for Free to come through as soon as he busted threw the door it was show time. Kairo was smart but he wasn't smarter than me. He thought because he was from Ethiopia that could move around without being touched. I heard Alexis arguing and Alonzo yelling saying let's go it was showtime.

"Air this bitch out. I want both of those niggas dead. Skeet and Khadir y'all roll with me. Ricky, you guard the front door take Giselle and Kassence outside. Boo, you get the back door. Alonzo, you know what to do. Mask off and handle your business." Alonzo ran up the stairs first and bum rushed Free. Dumb ass nigga didn't even see Alonzo coming I couldn't watch. I was right behind him. I wanted two things Journee and Kairo dead.

Alonzo

Juelz couldn't say air this bitch out quick enough for me. I had to get at Free the worst fucking way. I heard that nigga talking mad shit to Alexis. I was biting the inside of my jaw listening to that shit. I'm a street nigga that came from nothing. Alexis is the closest thing that I had to a girlfriend.

Free disrespected her not once but twice and today was the last fucking time. Free didn't even see me coming. I caught that pussy ass nigga off guard. He was all up in Alexis's face. I didn't even have the time to tell my niggas to get Giselle and her daughter out of the room. I was in straight go mode.

Journee had a vase sitting on her glass coffee table. I picked it up and swung it in that back of Free's head like it was a baseball bat. He stumbled to the ground. I picked him up and slammed him into the glass coffee table, glass was every fucking where. Back in the day, I use to break into houses. Anytime I heard glass shatter it was fucking showtime.

Free looked at me and I looked at him. He tried to get up. I wasn't about to give this nigga a chance to gain his composure. He had life fucked up. I went ape shit on his pussy ass with these hands. I gave that nigga straight head shots to his skull. I lit his jaw up. He was a bloody mess. I started stomping the shit out of him. I blacked out for a minute until Alexis told me she wanted to finish him off.

"Baby let me finish him please." I let Alexis do her thing. I've done enough. Free thought he was untouchable until he met a nigga like me.

Juelz

I ran up the stairs to Journee's room, the door was cracked open. I told Skeet and Khadir to stand down this shit didn't look right.

I had to do a double take. Kairo's pants were down and Journee's legs were thrown over his shoulders. No, she wouldn't do me like that. I crept into the room I came too far to turn around now. I heard her arguing and crying. He was talking shit.

"I can't wait for this nigga to see me fucking you and killing you. Bitch you gone die today."
I wanted to kill Kairo, and just get this shit over with. I told y'all the only light skin nigga I trust is Skeet. I couldn't just sit back and watch this nigga fuck my bitch. Killing Kairo was to fucking easy. He had to feel me before I send him off to his maker.

This nigga was taking the pussy she wasn't giving it up he took it. I noticed he had a gun pointed at Journee's head. I had to think and move quick. I walked up behind him. This nigga was too busy trying to bust a nut in my pussy to notice that I was behind him. Journee looked up at me. I put my hands up to my lips for her not to say shit.

"That pussy good ain't it? He reached for the gun. I kneed him and knocked the gun out of his hand really quick. He turned around an attempted fight me. I hit him with a quick jab to the jaw.

He hit me back. This nigga was starting to feel himself I wanted him too because I was going to rock his ass to sleep with these hands. He pulled his pants up that was my advantage.

As soon as he knelt down. I kicked him in his face and busted his mouth open instantly. Blood was everywhere. I picked him up and body slammed the fuck out of him. I wasn't satisfied. I turned him around, so he could face me. My fist connected with his jaw and skull numerous of times, he fell to the floor. I had to kill him with my bare hands. Journee jumped up and grabbed the gun from underneath her pillow she started emptying her clip in him and I did the same his body was lifeless. I took Journee's gun from her she looked at me and smiled.

"Juelz."

"Go take shower, right fucking now and wash that shit up off you."

"He raped me."

"I know Journee, but go clean up. Khadir and Skeet are outside of the door." Killing Kairo was too easy. The streets gave this nigga too much clout. Pussy will always be a nigga down fall especially my pussy.

He didn't even see me coming. I walked out of Journee's room. I couldn't stand the smell of him on her. I hope she doesn't need anything here because she's never coming back here to Africa or Ethiopia.

"Is she good."

"Yeah, Khadir she's good." I walked downstairs to see what Alonzo was up too, him and Alexis. I knew he made a mess and caused some damage.

"Alonzo, what the fuck man?" Free was laid on the floor with his mouth wide open and he was staring at the ceiling. The gun was stuck in between his mouth and his brains were laying on the floor.

"Juelz, I told you I was killing him the same way he did Alexis. Did you think I was bullshitting, this fuck nigga didn't want to see me? I thought we were at least going to shoot it out, he didn't even have a gun on him. I could've killed him with my bare hands, but I asked Alexis how did she want to handle him and she said to make his ass eat some lead, that's the way he did her. She's pregnant with my seed."

Alexis and Alonzo are both crazy as fuck. We had to dispose of these fuck niggas bodies quickly. Rick came in and said that Giselle and Kassence need to use that bathroom. I forgot all about Giselle and Kassence.

Free had to go Kassence would be fatherless. I'm a heartless ass nigga, but I would never want Kassence to see her father laid here dead.

Journee had a bathroom in her basement. Me, Skeet and Khadir and Alonzo started disposing of Free and Kairo's body. We had two body bags, the insides were doused with acid. It would eat their flesh alive.

"Where's the nearest river?"

"Little Blue Nile isn't too far from here."

"How far?"

"Juelz, we might need to find somewhere else to dump the body. We dumped five there today."

"Alexis, what the fuck y'all do?"

"We killed Tyra and her friends, she was fucking with Journee again. Your baby momma gave her nice shot right between her eyes."

"Oh okay." I need to speak with Journee about this. I can't get the image out of my head of her and Kairo fucking. I know he took the pussy but damn that shit got my head fucked up and it's playing with my mental.

Chapter -25

Journee

Juelz snuck up on me. He was sneaky that's why he wasn't answering the phone. Nikki played me. My heart dropped when Juelz caught Kairo taking the pussy. Thank God, the stroke of his dick didn't do anything for me. Juelz looked at me like he was disgusted. It was his fault anyway.

Nobody told him to kill Farrah and send him that shit. I stayed in the shower for as long as I could. I hope by the time the water turns cold I could step out and Kairo's body is gone. I hated that Kairo had to die, but damn he took shit too far.

I gave this man eight years of my life. Never in a million years, I would've thought we would be here. We built a beautiful and nice life together. He was my king and I was his queen. This man was living a double life. I loved him I honestly felt that he would've killed me to prove a point.

He loved his mother. What would I do without Juelz? I don't even want to find out. I heard a knock on that bathroom door.

"Come in."

"You're running all the hot water out ain't you."

"Yep, my mind is in overdrive."

"I know I heard you caught a few bodies earlier."

"Who told you, Alexis or Giselle?"

"Alexis."

"Juelz, why didn't you tell me that you were coming? I was worried about you."

"I wanted to surprise you, but I didn't know that I was going to catch him fucking you."

"Juelz, you know that I would never fuck him off the strength that I'm pregnant with your child and we have something that we're trying to pursue. He took the pussy I didn't give it to him."

"Why were you naked? He undressed you."

"I was in the shower and he yanked me out, and threw me on the bed. You don't believe me, do you? Why am I even explaining myself?" I can't believe Juelz right now. I know what it looks like but that's not what it was. I didn't enjoy him fucking me. I had plenty of chances to fuck Kairo, but I wasn't pressed for the dick that belonged to him.

I'm ready to go home. I pushed passed Juelz and threw some clothes on. Kairo's blood was still on my floor. I wanted to see my brother and Skeet. Juelz is crazy as fuck. We may be better off co-parenting.

Alexis

Free busted in here like a mad man. He jacked me up and threw me on the couch and told me he was going to kill me since we had his momma killed. I never liked Farrah fuck that bitch and she never liked me. I was glad that she was dead. I heard Kairo yelling at Journee, me and Giselle were trying to think of a plan to get him out of here. Kassence was already nervous.

Baby, when Alonzo ran up them, steps from the basement and busted in like he was Tony Montana my heart skipped a beat. My baby was on go, he had his dreads pulled back in a ponytail. My nigga was suited. He ran up on Free and smashed his in the back of his head. They started tussling. I grabbed the gun from underneath the couch pillow.

I ran up behind Free and smashed him on the side of his face with my gun. He was in a daze. Alonzo started boxing his ass out he fell to the floor quick. Alonzo asked me how did I want to kill him and I told him. Free deserved to die. He was a heartless monster. I haven't seen Journee yet. I walked toward her room and she was rushing out. I grabbed her I could tell that she was pissed.

"What's wrong?"

"You don't want to know Alexis."

"Enlighten me." Juelz walked passed, and she turned her head to avoid eye contact with him.

"Alexis, he walked in and Kairo's pants were down his dick was in my pussy. He took the pussy. Juelz heard him say that. He's mad about it. I didn't know Farrah was dead."

"Are you serious Journee? Kairo was that desperate to take it. Juelz's knows better."

"Alexis at this point I don't fucking care anymore. The only thing that I want to do is see my brother. Go home and see my daughter and turn myself in that's it. I've been through so much these past few months. I'm done explaining myself to niggas. Fuck them and leave me the fuck alone."

"Journee I'm here for you no matter what. Put yourself in his shoes, how would you react? He'll get over it."

"Alexis, females ain't raping niggas period and taking dick like that." Journee wasn't hearing anything that I had to say. Juelz knew better, they'll work through their issues like they work through everything else. They've come too far to go two steps backwards. I can't wait to love and fuck on Alonzo. I thought this moment would never come.

Chapter-26

Giselle

Well, I guess our time in Ethiopia is almost up. Juelz, Alonzo and Skeet and their crew busted up in Journee's compound like some real live animals. Juelz's cousin Ricky and this guy named Dro ushered me and Kassence outside into a car.

I knew what time it was. I didn't want to come to terms with it, but it is what it is. I'm a single mother now. I had access to all of Free's money and off shore accounts. The Porsche truck that he brought me I need that shipped back over to my home. Kassence and me will forever be straight.

I've been through so much these past few months. Every lesson was a blessing. I've made plenty of mistakes in my life. I've grown a lot over these past few months. I've been walking around out here blind for so long. It took for me to be taken out of my comfort zone to realize what life is about.

I'm the last one standing, some may think that I don't deserve to still be here amongst the living. That may be true, but everybody deserves a second chance. I'm not perfect and I know God is still working on me. I'm a work in progress. I'm very thankful that Journee and Alexis for not giving up on me when I gave up on myself.

They had my back when a man and female who I considered my sister and best friend didn't.

I don't know what the future may hold for us when we get back to Atlanta, but it is what it is. We may not be besties, but I wouldn't mind seeing the two of them occasionally. I would definitely miss Momma Edith dearly.

Journee and Alexis encouraged me to go to school for hair because I could do hair really good. They insisted that I open up a salon. Tyra never encouraged me to do shit but lay on my back and get paid. I didn't even know how to cook. They taught me how to cook a few things.

I would have to do better for my daughter. Free was gone and Juelz was no longer around. I didn't have to cook or do anything but just clean. This trip wasn't the best experience, but it was a learning experience. Kassence and I were still in the basement waiting for them to come and get us.

The basement door opened, and it was Momma Edith.

"My child I'm going to miss you and my granddaughter. Please keep in touch with me."

"Don't make me cry. I'm going to miss you so much."

"You'll be just fine my child. Hold your head up high. Keep your crown straight.

I love you and God loves you. People may judge you, but so what nobody's perfect. It's not about how you start it's about how you finish. Believe in yourself and have faith. I'll be checking on you."

"I love you too momma. It's going to be so hard. I've gotten used to having you around. I don't have anybody but God, Kassence, my mother, and grandmother, but I'll be all right."

"You'll be fine they'll come around."

"Who is they?"

"Journee and Alexis."

"I doubt it, but I'm okay with that. They've done more than enough. I need to work on me anyway."

"Don't be like that Giselle stop being so hard on yourself. Let it go all of it. The three of you bonded here. It's a reason that the three of y'all are here together and went through this."

"I here you mother. Lock my number in and pray they don't kill me."

"My child hush, if that was the case, you would've been dead already." Somebody else was knocking at the door. It was the guy Dro.

"Giselle, you and your daughter can come up now."

"Thanks, Dro will be up in a minute I need to finish speaking with my mother."

"Mother I think this maybe our goodbye. Please keep in touch with me. Kassence give grandmother hug before we leave."

"My child, that man there is your future husband."

"Momma stop, how do you know?"

"I just know I noticed the way he looked at you when he ushered you and Kassence to the car. Even just now I noticed the way he looked at you."

"Mother I'm not ready for a relationship right now."

"That may be true but if he's looking for the friendship be his friend and if he wants to put you back together again let him do just that. Listen to me my child, and take my words to heart. I know a few things and in short period of time I've taught you a lot and I'll continue to teach you. Go with the flow that's all I'm saying."

"Ok momma I'm listening." Lord Momma Edith is a mess this man is my future husband. We'll see he is easy on the eyes and I can't deny it. Kassence and I said our final goodbye to Momma Edith and made our way upstairs to prepare for this journey ahead of us.

Journee

My time in Ethiopia is up. I wasn't selling my house here. I'll be back but I don't know when. I loved it here despite our recent circumstances. I said my final goodbye to Momma Edith I would miss her dearly. Juelz had two SUV's parked out front that we got in. We headed toward the Little Blue Nile to dump Kairo and Free's body.

I tried to get into the one with Giselle and he grabbed me and put me in the one with him. We pulled off and headed to the boat docks, so we could travel back to Somalia. Me, Alexis, Alonzo, Skeet, and Juelz were in one SUV. Giselle and Kassence were in the other SUV. I kind of wanted her in here with us because she was the only female in there.

Alonzo and Alexis were making up for lost times. I sat behind Juelz and he sat in front of me. I promise you I didn't think us reuniting would be like this. Sometimes shit just ain't meant to be and I've ignored the signs, but it is what it is. Besides that, killing Kairo was heavy on the mind.

***

Three hours later we made it back to Somalia the boat ride was nice. It was so hot and humid the waves of the ocean were deep and just the thought of being free was amazing.

I couldn't enjoy it like I wanted too because Juelz and I were at odds. I'm sure everybody could fill the tension between the two of us it was ridiculous.

Khadir sat next to me and we caught up. I had to ask him about this new leading lady that was in his life that I knew nothing about. Her name was Regan and I couldn't wait to meet her. He told me that Khadijah was pregnant which I knew nothing about and Godmother Valerie was the one that killed Kairo's mother. I should've known she doesn't play any games period.

Juelz rented a house for a week in Somalia I didn't want to stay here for a week maybe a day or two, but I was ready to go home and see my princess. I haven't seen Jueleez in weeks and that's too long. The driver pulled up to the house. It was nice it wasn't too far from Pure's condo. Juelz unlocked the door, and everybody followed suit.

Kassence ran up to me and asked me could she sleep with me. Giselle ran up behind her and told her not tonight. I told Giselle that we would have to work out something out because Kassence is hooked on me and she refuses to let me out of her sight.

Alexis and Alonzo grabbed them a room. Giselle and Kassence had a room. I told Khadir that I was sleeping in his room. Juelz grabbed me and pushed me in his room. I don't know why he was doing all of this. I didn't want to be around him right now, and I would probably say some shit that I would regret.

Instead of having a conversation with Juelz right now. I went to the bathroom and took another hot shower. My mind was all over the place and I wanted to be alone. I heard the bathroom door open and it was him. I thought he was just using the bathroom and leaving. To my surprise, he got in the shower with me. He tapped me on my shoulder. I refused to turn around.

"Journee."

"Juelz."

"Look I'm sorry. The last thing that I want to see is any nigga touching you that's not me. Do you forgive me?"

"Yes, but you should know me better than that." Juelz and I continued to shower. I was tired and I'm sure he could tell that I was. We dried off. Juelz carried me to the bed and I laid on his chest. This is the only place that I wanted to be right here with him. We drifted off to sleep.

Giselle

We finally made it to Somalia. Dro kept his eyes trained on me the whole time. He made me feel uncomfortable. Journee and Juelz were mad at each other for some reason, but that shit didn't last long. They deserve each other she's a good girl and he's a great guy. If that's what love looks like.

I can't wait until a man loves me the way he loves her. I don't know how I missed it, but he never looked at me that way. He was so attentive to her it was crazy. You can't deny their chemistry. I put Kassence to bed she's was tired we had a long day.

I took a hot shower and slipped on some pajamas. I went to the kitchen to grab me something to drink. It was a patio outside I needed to go sit out there for a few minutes to get my mind right and meditate. No one was on the patio that was perfect. I sat with my eyes closed for at least ten minutes.

I heard that patio door open. I didn't think anything of it. Someone sat next to me and his cologne smelled familiar. I know Creed cologne from anywhere.

"Do you mind if I join you?"

"No, your fine." He's freaking me out now, damn are you stalking me or something?

"My name is Roderick Shannon, but you can call me Dro."

"It's nice to meet you I'm Giselle Lawrence." He extended his hand out for me to shake.

"What's your story beautiful? I notice that you're the only female out here that doesn't have a man. May I ask why?"

"What makes you think that I have a story? I'm single for many reasons."

"My mother always told me, the eyes were the keys to a women's soul. Your eyes have a story. I can see the hurt and the pain begging to be freed. You move with caution it's so noticeable."

"You said a mouthful, your mother may know a few things."

"What did he do?"

"They did a lot, nothing that I care to share. With time all wounds would heal, but I'll be all right." I started crying and I didn't even realize it. He stood in front of me and wiped my tears.

"I'm sorry beautiful I didn't mean to pry or make you cry."

"It's cool I'm learning to let go of a lot of things, and crying is releasing."

"Do you live in Atlanta?"

"I do."

"Can I take you out on a date?"

"Roderick, are you seeing anyone? I'm not in the business of dealing with someone that's seeing or on the dating scene."

"I had someone that I was interested in we were good for each other, but she had a situation that was bigger than us and I couldn't compare to that. We had to let each other go."

"She must have been special they way you spoke about her. Your face lit up."

"She was special to me, but she's married with twins and she has another child on the way."

"Oh, so she was the one that got way?"

"No, she was never mine, to begin with. She had a situation that was before my time. Six years in the making. We crossed paths, and we started dating, but time was never on our side. When I met her she was pregnant with twins? I stayed down with her through her pregnancy until she had her babies.

Her husband refused to let anybody get next to her. He proposed, and it was a wrap. It was best that she went her way and I went mine because her husband and I would've bumped heads if we took it there."

"She seems like she was special, and she had the best of both worlds."

"Kaniya was special to me, in a perfect world we could be together, but Lucky staked his claim to her a long ago, and he was willing to die behind that pussy excuse my language. I had to step aside and let them do them. Enough about me what about you Giselle?"

"What would you like to know?"

"Everything."

"Why?"

"Because I'm trying to get to know you."

"Why do you want to know me?"

"I just do."

"Look, Roderick, I'm a mess and I'm working on myself right now."

"I understand. I'm a mess too, but let me help you work through your mess and put you back together again." For the remainder of the night, Dro and I sat up and talked about everything up under the sun. He was from the Southside too. I enjoyed his conversation. He told me that he had two sons also, but he was single and not dating.

***

Chapter -27

Juelz

We made it back to the states Jueleez was so happy to see her mother. I was happy for her. I couldn't stay mad at Journee for long. I had to get over that shit quick. She was in her feelings. I knew that Journee would never cheat on me. I was still pissed because I couldn't eat her and fuck her all night like I wanted too.

Journee was scheduled to turn herself in on Monday. My attorney said that she should be good. I hope so because Kairo was dead and without him there was no case. I needed her free and clear. I made her move in with me, she wanted to go home.

Her new home was with me and Jueleez. She wanted to see Nikki and Khadijah, but I told her she could go see them in a few days. Jueleez missed her and I did too. I'm a selfish ass nigga and I wasn't letting her out of my sight not even for a minute.

"Baby what if they keep me?"

"Journee, you're good they just want to ask you a few questions that's it."

"Okay if you say so."

"I know so."

"Why can't I go to Nikki's house?"

"Because daddy missed you that's why. You have plenty of time to go to Nikki's house, but right now I need all your time. I missed you."

"Let you tell it. How much did you miss me?"

"Let me show you." Journee already knew what time it was. I don't know why she liked playing with me. Nikki and Skeet need to spend their time together. I already had to make Smoke keep Khadijah at home she's been trying to sneak over here. I'm real close to telling Journee about her and Khadir. Smoke told me that Nikki told him that she believes that Khadijah is selling dope.

I couldn't stress Journee out with Khadijah's mess because she's pregnant with my son. I'm claiming a boy and I would be good.

Journee

We made it back home safe. The twenty-four flight wasn't bad we stopped in Dubai to drop Juelz cousin Ricky off and his two friends, this was my first time meeting him. I wanted to stay in Dubai for a few days, but I didn't have my passport because I was kidnapped. That really sucked because I wanted to get my passport stamped. Dubai is a very strict country.

I made sure to ask Juelz what was going on because I wanted to know how did he have access to the plane. He told me that he owned it and his old connect gave it to him as a parting gift. I hope that was the case because I couldn't get caught up in anymore illegal shit. He assured me that was through with the game and he's been through for more than a few years.

We stayed in Somalia for only a day. I hung out with Pure, Eboni and Majesty because who knows when the next time that I would back or see them again. I'm so glad that Juelz and I made up the other night. I laid on his chest all night and he whispered sweet nothings in my ear.

His touch alone did something to me. I wanted to fuck him so bad. He hasn't touched me at since he saw me with Kairo. My pussy was throbbing to be freed, fucking with Kairo's dumb deranged ass. The moment I laid eyes on Jueleez she ran up and hugged me and placed her tiny hands on my stomach.

I missed her so much. I wanted to kick with Momma Simone for a few hours, but Juelz had other plans. He took me to his house. I told him that I at least wanted to go by the house to check on a few things.

He told me that there is nothing to check on. I asked him what did he mean by that. He said we're living together.

Of course, I wanted to wake up to him every day, but damn check with me first before you just up and make the decision to pack my shit and move me in your house. I've been cooped up in this house with him and Jueleez I didn't mind it one bit. I wanted to see Nikki and Khadijah.

I haven't heard from Alexis at all. I think I might do a family dinner at my house on Sunday since I'm turning myself in on Monday. Everything should go smoothly hopefully. I still haven't told Juelz that Kairo left me everything that he had. I'm not sure if I want to or not.

"Mommy, can we make a pan of brownies?"

"Sure baby, go pick out some."

Chapter-28

Nikki

Journee has been back for about three days now, and I haven't seen her or heard from her.

I'm about this close from riding over Juelz house and popping off. I called Alexis and she was acting all nonchalant. She told me that she was pregnant. Congratulations I'm another Godmother. I'm just saying who was about to watch these kids, and be in the delivery room? Her and Khadijah are due around the same time.

I wanted to know who all got killed, and how was Giselle still alive? Last, I knew she was the enemy. I couldn't ask Skeet. He wouldn't give me all the details like I needed, fuck that I'm impatient ass female. I couldn't stand the suspense it's killing me. My mother has called me twenty times wanting to know what happened over there.

"Skeet I'll be back."

"Where are you going, Nikki?"

"Juelz house, I need to see Journee fuck space. It's been three days already and I can't take it."

"The kids and I will come and ride with you."

"Oh, you want to ride with me today, but you know I've been wanting to go over there. Skeet you got me fucked up. Keep your ass at home."

"Nikki, watch your fucking mouth. I've been real patient and lenient with you. Damn Juelz just wanted a few days to himself."

"How are you being patient with me Skeet? I can't call Journee or go see her. I don't give a fuck what Juelz wants, that hasn't stopped the two of y'all chopping it up every day."

"Nikki chill out, let's go I'm not even about start arguing with you right now. You're making shit harder than what it is. Watch how you talk to me. I'm the man in this house and last, I checked I slang cock and not you. I let you get away with too much shit around here."

"Whatever Skeet."

"Don't whatever me." I don't know what Skeet's problem is, but him and Juelz both have me fucked up. I don't care how much cock he slangs around here. He can keep slanging it. He wanted to ride with me, he can drive too.

"Lil Skeet and Nyla let's go. Skeet you can drive." He loaded the kids up. I took my precious time getting in the car. I brought Journee the new iPhone X since she didn't have time to preorder it.

I got in the car with Skeet and slammed the door. I knew he wanted to say something smart so bad, but he couldn't because the kids are in the car. I laughed hysterically.

"Momma you crazy."

"I know Lil Skeet your daddy forgot." Skeet grabbed my leg and started squeezing it.

***

We finally made it to Journee and Juelz's house. I didn't even let Skeet put the car in park good before I jumped out. I banged on the door like I was the God damn police. Juelz swung the door open with a scowl on his face.

"Move you know why I'm here." I didn't even say hey. I moved his ass right out the way. I didn't come to see him. I came to see Journee Leigh, I smelled something coming from out the kitchen. I knew she was cooking some beef stew it smelled so damn good. I made my way toward the kitchen and there she was.

"Nikki, I knew that was you banging on the door like the fucking police. No damn home training."

"Good because I missed you believe or not." Lil Skeet and Nyla ran into the kitchen and gave Journee a hug. It was good to see my bitch in the flesh. I had to look her over to make sure that she was untouched. The kids went to go play with Jueleez. Journee made me a bowl of beef stew and some butter milk cornbread.

"So where can we talk?"

"I have a woman's cave. Why did you and Khadijah let Juelz pack my shit up?"

"Journee, I didn't let Juelz do shit. You know how he is." Journee and I finished eating. We went inside of her woman's cave to talk. I need the tea play for play.

"Spill it bitch what happened? Here I got you the iPhone X you can thank me later." Journee started explaining everything that happened. I couldn't believe any of this shit. My bitch caught two bodies in one day and the nigga took the pussy and died afterwards. Kairo was crazy as fuck. I'm mad that I wasn't with her. How did Journee catch a body before me?

"So why is Giselle alive again?"

"It's a long story, Nikki."

"Bitch I got time. Explain it I can spend the night if need be." Journee started explaining everything that happened. I had to cut her off.

"Who in the fuck is Momma Edith, and why is she running around saving hoes. Project Pat stopped doing that years ago."

"Nikki, chill out. It's Pure, Eboni, and Majesty's mom."

"Girl you need to stop hanging with them Africans." It was good seeing Journee I missed her so much.

"Enough about me Nikki what about you, what's been going on with you?"

"Girl I thought you would never ask. I have so much shit to tell you. Let me tell you about your little sister and brother first."

"What about them?"

"I'm not for certain about Khadijah, but she has some involvement. Khadir is the fucking plug."

"You a damn lie. I swear to God on my mother if Khadir is selling drugs I'm going to turn his world upside down. Where's he getting the work from?"

"Big KD who else. I meant to tell you a few weeks ago. Khadijah is doing something too. She had two duffle bags full of money, nothing but big face hundreds. It smelled like straight Pyrex. She said she was counting the money for Big KD. She wouldn't even let me come in her house that day.

"Oh really." Journee and I finished catching up. We Facetimed my momma and she was going slap off. Nyla and Lil Skeet asked could they spend the night. I told Juelz that Lil Skeet needs his own room because at Journee's house he had his own everything.

Skeet and I would be home all alone tonight. You know what that means fucking until the sun comes up. Skeet's been mad at me lately because he wants another child because everybody has a baby on the way except for him.

We already have two, how many more does he want? Years ago, he told me that he wanted five.

I thought he was just bullshitting. We pulled off from Journee and Juelz's house. Skeet looked at me and I looked at him. He was waiting for me to say something.

"What, why are you looking at me like that?"

"You know why."

"I don't."

"Okay." If Skeet was looking for an apology, he wasn't about to get one from me. I don't see anything that I've done wrong. My girls and I couldn't all be pregnant at the same time. If some shit was to pop off, somebody had to tag a few bitches.

***

We made it home in about twenty minutes. Normally when Skeet and I are alone just the two of us. I'll give him so slow head while he drives, but I'm petty and my lips ain't touching shit today. We pulled up in the garage. I hopped out and made my way to our bedroom. I wanted to take a nice hot shower and relax. Skeet was right on my heels, he stopped me at the entrance of our bedroom door.

He grabbed me by my waist. I looked at him over my shoulder. He kissed me.

"You want me to fuck you up huh?"

"No Skeet, leave me alone. Let me take a shower." I entered the bathroom I stripped naked and adjusted the water temperature in the shower. It was just right. Steam started to cover the mirror. I stepped in and lathered with Caress Body wash. I wasn't even in the shower a good five minutes.

Skeet came in the shower with me naked as the day he was born dick swinging everywhere. He grabbed the soap and started to wash himself up. His dick kept tapping me on my ass. I ignored him and attempted to get out. He grabbed me, and I looked at him.

"Handle that."

"Handle what Skeet?" He knew I was playing dumb.

"I told you I slang good cock, right?" I nodded my head yes. Skeet picked me up and slammed me on dick, he started fucking me senseless. He pressed my back up against the base of the shower for support. I wrapped my arms around his neck.

"Take this dick." I started bouncing on his dick and riding the shit out of him, I was draining his ass tonight.

"You're having my baby."

Chapter-29

Giselle

Kassence and I have been at home for about four days now. I gave Journee and Alexis both my number both to reach out to me. I contacted Momma Edith immediately. I needed to figure out how to get my Porsche truck shipped over here. I left her the keys. She called me and said that she was arranging to have it shipped over here. I should have it within four days. She sent me an email with the instructions on where to pick my truck up from.

I couldn't leave that truck in Ethiopia. I've been talking to Dro lately heavy on the phone. It felt like I was a teenager again. He wanted to take me out on a date. I'm a little skeptical about dating so soon because I'm working on myself. I vowed to give Kassence more time than I ever had. She's been asking about Free lately. I couldn't tell her the truth now, but I would later.

He abandoned us, even when he came to Journee's house he didn't acknowledge us, that sealed the deal and hurt my heart and soul. I'm also taking Momma Edith's advice wisely. I've fucked the wrong niggas countless of times, and I hope Dro would be my Mr. Right. For some reason, I believed Momma Edith. It just felt different this time, his vibe was different, and he was open.

I didn't have a baby sitter. Dro said his mom could watch Kassence for me. It was way too soon for that. My mom and grandmother went to the casino this weekend. I didn't have anybody to call, so I called Journee to see what she thinks.

"Yo."

"Journee."

"Giselle."

"Are you busy, can you talk?"

"Of course, what's up?"

"I have a date tonight, but I don't have a baby sitter. I'm working on myself. I enrolled in school I start in December, and the only reason that I'm considering is that Momma Edith said that he's my future husband. I'm curious."

"Giselle, who is it damn stop beating around the bush and tell me."

"Dro."

"Dro from the trip, Alonzo's homeboy?"

"Yes."

"Well damn, Momma Edith might not be lying. Do you want me to get Kassence for you? I'm taking Jueleez and my two God children to Sky Zone, she could come with us."

"You would do that for me?"

"Yes, bring her to my house in Bankhead. Do you remember where it's at? We should be back by 9:00 pm, but I'll call you when we make it back."

"Thank you, send me the address please?"

***

I got Kassence dressed and dropped her off with Journee. Nikki was giving me the side eye. Nikki never liked me, she knew Kassence wasn't Juelz daughter Kassence loved her dearly, she used to play with Nyla all the time. Alexis was with them also she threw her hand up also.

Nikki was probably in her ear, but Journee didn't care about the past. She was real, and I loved that about her. She came through for me. Dro and I had dinner reservations at Legal Seafood. We had reservations at 7:00 pm.

It was a thirty-minute drive. I made it there on time. It was a black Bentley coupe parked next to me. I didn't think anything of it. I walked in believe or not I was dressed casually. When I got back home I purchased me a few pairs of jeans and some cute tennis shoes. My outfit consisted of some distressed Calvin Klein Jeans and a white blouse, navy blue blazer. I paired it with some Navy-Blue Jessica Simpson pumps.

As soon as I stepped up to the waiter to give her my name for the reservation. I smelled him. He walked up behind me and put his arm around my waist.

"Shannon two please, we have reservations."

"You're early."

"Always, these are for you."

"Thank you, they're beautiful." He brought me a dozen white roses. Dro was a real gentleman. I couldn't tell you the last time I received flowers. I'm nervous. He was talking a good game.

"Talk to me beautiful."

"What do you want to talk about?"

"You of course. I want to know the real you."

"Why, what makes you want to know about me?"

"Why not you?" I've been contemplating on if I wanted to divulge the real me to Dro. What you see is what you get. The only thing that I regret is leading Juelz on and making him think that Kassence was his, and continuing to pursue Free while he was with Alexis. I began to tell Dro everything about me.

He was listening and holding my hands as I was speaking. He was staring at me I couldn't take it. I started to get up and leave. He slid in and sat right next to me. He wrapped his arms around me.

"Giselle, I got you all of you. I didn't bring you here to judge you or upset you. I'm not trying to get to know you to hurt you.

You've been through a lot and you've got it wrong a few times, but that's okay. I know I'm not perfect but I'm more than worth it. I don't want to be your wrong. I want to be your right. Promise me you'll give us a fair shot."

"I will." Dro was a man of many words. We talked and ate our food for the remainder of the night. It was getting late and I had to pick up Kassence from Journee's. Dro walked me to the car. He pinned me up against the door and gave me a kiss. I tried to pull back, but he wouldn't let me. He's aggressive and I like that about him. I smiled because he was a great kisser.

"I've been wanting to do that to you for a few days now. I think you needed that kiss."

"Thank you for the kiss. I have to get going."

"Alright, that's cool call me when you make it home." Dro kissed me on my forehead and watched me pull off. Journee's house was about forty-five minutes from here. I made it at exactly 9:00 pm. I sent Journee a text to let her know I was pulling, she said that they were around the corner and they would be pulling up in a few minutes.

Journee pulled up ten minutes later. Nikki and Alexis pulled off. Jueleez and Kassence came to the car door.

"Mommy, Journee said you can come in." I got out of the car and Jueleez just stared at me.

"Hi, Ms. Giselle."

"Hi, Jueleez." Her name didn't do her any justice. She was her father's child. She looks exactly like him.

"You could've come in Giselle."

"Journee, Nikki doesn't like me, she never has and Alexis her wave was a little too dry for my liking so I'm good."

"Alexis is pregnant, she's a moody chic right now. Nikki is Nikki she'll come around."

"Whose Alexis pregnant by?"

"Not Free, Alonzo."

"Alonzo has always been crazy, and Alexis is crazy too the perfect couple." I laughed.

"How was your date?"

"It was amazing and nice, he was the perfect gentleman. His conversation was grown, but I don't know.

"You're glowing! He might be the one. Time heals all wounds."

"Journee, I'm so scared, my trust is fucked up and I've been hurt one too many times. I've picked the wrong guy more than once, and I don't want to do that again. I don't know what's right."

"Just take it one day at a time. When you find Mr. Right he'll be completely different than what you're used to. It'll feel different."

"He feels different." Journee and I talked for a few more minutes after that Kassence and I headed home. Dro was heavy on the mind."

Chapter-30

Journee

It's been a long week; Tomorrow I was scheduled to turn myself in. Juelz hired me an attorney. I had my own attorney also. She knew the business relationship that Kairo and I had. Everything that we had together was legit. I still haven't had the time to sit down and let Juelz know that Kairo left me everything.

This is a hard conversation to have with him, but I must be open and honest with him. Once I broke up with Kairo after the whole Tyra situation. I was in the process of getting everything dissolved. Kairo left me with everything he owned was rightfully mine on paper. He had millions and I'm not talking one or two.

On paper Kairo had one hundred million dollars in assets, that just consists of the clean money I'm not attached too. Together we have twenty-five million dollars in assets. He also has money stashed in off shore accounts. He has drug empire that's worth millions. Kairo had two trap phones. I had one and he had one. He gave me one in case there was an emergency or if anything happened to him.

He wanted me to assist Free with the day to day operations with the Hussein Mafia. Free and Kairo are both dead. I'm the plug by default. I wanted to live a normal life. I didn't want to be bothered with any of this shit. Kairo needed to die, but damn this was the last thing that I thought about when killing him came to mind.

I laid my head on my desk in my office. I was still in a fucked-up situation with Kairo dead.

"What's wrong?" I looked up and it was Juelz standing in the doorway smiling at me. Damn, he was sexy. He called himself teasing me about some females wanting him to do the gray sweat pants challenge. I put my gray sweat pants on and told him to upload my picture, so the guys could see this print between my legs. He tried to kill me.

"Everything."

"You want to talk about it?"

"I need to, but I don't want too."

"Talk to me what's up?" Juelz walked up to me and picked me up out of me seat. He carried me over to the sectional that was in my woman cave and laid me down on his chest. He started to smother me with his kisses.

"Juelz, I don't know how to say this."

"Say it, baby, I'm listening." He bit my bottom lip and started sucking on it.

"I'm the plug."

"Plug?"

"We killed Kairo, he left me everything, including his drug empire."

"Journee, I don't want you fucking with that shit period."

"Juelz, don't you think I know that?"

"Kairo was involved in a lot of shit that you know nothing about. To be honest Journee don't touch any of the assets until your free and clear of everything. The FEDS can drop a case and pick it back up at any time. I need to make sure your name is clear, and they can't recharge you."

"My attorney said my case will be dismissed with prejudice." Juelz and I talked for the rest of the night. We picked out baby colors he swears it's a boy. I hope so because I wasn't doing this again.

***

Monday finally snuck up on me. I had to turn myself in Nikki and Alexis met me at the courthouse. Juelz, Skeet and Khadir and God momma Valerie came also. Alonzo said that he wasn't coming any where near a Federal building. I understood where he was coming from. Juelz and I, and my Attorney's went to meet with the Federal prosecutors.

The prosecutors looked me up and down. They laid all the evidence that they were accusing me of. Nothing was concrete.

"Ms. Armstrong, you evaded arrest."

"No sir I was kidnapped."

"Why wasn't it reported."

"My family didn't think that I was in danger because of our former relationship." The prosecutors began to ask question after question in hopes of catching me in a lie of some sort. They asked me a lot of things about Kairo that I didn't know the answer too. Thank God that I didn't know anything because I would incriminate myself.

"What was the sole purpose of you resolving all of your assets? A witness stated that you were involved in Mr. Hussein's drug empire."

"I never knew anything about any drugs. The only business that we acquired together was the real estate." My attorney answered the remaining questions and provided my financial records. All charges were dismissed. They asked did I know the whereabouts of Kairo. I told them he was in Ethiopia.

Juelz and I walked out hand in hand. I'm glad this over and put behind me. I just want to live a normal life with my kids and Juelz. They can have the cars, clothes, and fame I'm good on it. I gave my family the good news. We decided to go get some lunch I was starving.

Chapter-31

Khadijah

I guess think the neighbors think I'm selling dope

Motherfucka I am

I am

Selling dope, selling dope

Life is great minus the bullshit. I know it's early, but I love the Neighbors song by J. Cole. Journee has been home for almost a week. I haven't seen her or heard from her. I think she was mad at me. Every time I would call her she would sound so nonchalant and dry. I'm not sure what was behind it, but I wasn't feeling it.

I had a doctor's appointment today at 12:00 pm. Smoke said that he would meet me there. I wanted my sister to go with me, but she had to turn herself in. I prayed that everything worked out for her just fine. My clothes were already picked out. I had to fix me some breakfast really quick I was starving.

I heard my doorbell ring. I looked through the peep hole and I didn't see anybody. I didn't pay it no mind I continued to fix my breakfast. I heard a loud thud. I looked toward the living room by the door was being kicked in. I tried to grab my gun, but I was to slow for them. Oh, my God, I was being robbed. The robber was dressed in all black he had a ski mask on and gloves and pacer in his mouth his voice was muffled.

"Aye check the basement and upstairs. I want the money and the dope."

"I don't have anything."

"Bitch did I tell you to fucking talk? Lie again and I will blow your fucking brains out. I heard you work for Big KD." Tears ran down my face. I was being handcuffed and hog tied.

"Boss mane, she has a lean factory in the basement."

"Bag that shit up."

"Boss mane, she has stacks stuffed in that mattress." The other robber yelled they were taking everything that I fucking had.

"Take every fucking thing. I hate lying ass bitches they deserve to die. You can do it my way or learn the hard way."

"Can you please let me go?"

"Nah I came for the dope, and I'm not leaving without that. Everything else was extra."

"I don't have any."

"I hate liars, and for that, your lying ass is going to die today." He smacked my face hard and duct taped my mouth. He threw me over his shoulders and carried me upstairs to my room. The two other guys were headed downstairs with all my shit. Khadir was going to kill me. It was something about one of the robbers he looked familiar.

The robber threw me on my bed and handcuffed me. He grabbed his gun from behind his waist and cocked it back He was about to kill me. I never thought I would go out like this. I thought I would die by natural causes. He snatched the duct tape off my lips. It hurts so bad.

"Do you have anything to say before I kill you?"

"I'm pregnant."

"And."

"I'll tell you where the drugs are."

"Where are they?"

"How do I know that you won't kill me?"

"You'll have to find out and see."

"Inside of the floor."

"Does your child's father know what you're involved in?"

"No."

"Why not?"

"He wouldn't understand."

"What would he say if you and his child ended up dead?"

"He'll be livid."

"It's your fault." The robber got the drugs underneath my floor and the extra money I had hidden. He climbed on top of my body and cocked his gun back and pointed to my head. Tears flooded my face. I started breathing real heavy. I begged for my life.

"Please don't do this." He didn't say anything the gun was still trained on my head. He took off his pacemaker and gloves. He took his ski mask off and stared me in the eyes with so much hate.

"Smoke."

"Khadijah."

"Let me explain."

"Nope let me explain, shut the fuck up and listen. When we first got together. I told you I had you. I didn't want you selling drugs because as your man. I can handle all your needs, but this shit right here is a smack in my face. Do you see how easy it was for me to get at you?

"Khadijah you're not built for this shit. If this was a real home invasion you would've been dead on sight. If the FEDS swarmed in here today you would've been doing some real FED time. For that reason alone, I can't fuck with you Khadijah it's over.

If it's not about my seed you're carrying, don't hit me at all. It's a wrap. I can't trust you.

"I'm sorry Smoke. I love you don't do this to us."

"You did this to us."

"Don't walk out on us, Smoke I'm sorry I'll quit."

"Don't quit because of me leaving. Quit because you want too. When you have the baby, I'm taking my son." Smoke walked out on me and everything we had.

He untied me and left. My chest caved in. I was crying hysterically. I fucked up and I'm sorry. I regret it. I called my sister my heart can't take it.

"Journee, I need you he left me." I cried.

"Who, calm down Khadijah."

"Smoke."

Smoke

What you do in the dark, it always comes to the light. I hated to do Khadijah like that, but I had to. I had to hurt her to show her that she's not built for this shit. I've known for a minute that she was still up to this shit. When we made it official she told me that she wasn't doing it anymore.

Khadijah had no reason to hustle. She worked and anything that she wanted I can provide for her. She was being real reckless with the shit. She had every drug you can think of in her home. Never bring your work home to where you lay your head at.

I took all the drugs and gave it to Khadir. The money I dumped half of it into Khadijah's bank account. I opened a MMA account and dumped the other half in there. I went to speak with Big KD. I didn't want Khadijah involved in anything drug related. She just witnessed first-hand what Journee went through.

My phone was blowing up. It was my mother and Journee. Khadijah will be all right she needs to get ready for her doctor's appointment. What doesn't kill you makes you stronger. I'll be back to check on her. I love her, and she needed to see how dangerous this shit it. I scared her ass straight. My momma kept calling my phone. I had to answer.

"Yes, mother."

"Smoke, I don't know what the fuck you did to Khadijah, but you better fix this shit now. I didn't raise you to walk out on your family."

"Momma it's nothing like that."

"Well, what is it?"

"What did she tell you?"

"Does it matter?"

"Yes, I can't say that shit on the phone."

"Bye momma."

Chapter-32

Journee

My day went from good to worse. Khadijah called me crying hysterically. I didn't know what the fuck was going on. I hopped in the car with Alexis and Nikki immediately. My sister needed me, she was pregnant, and she shouldn't be that upset.

We pulled up to Khadijah's house and her door was kicked off the hinges that alone let me know that something was wrong. I ran in her house looking for her. It was ransacked.

"Khadijah, where are you?" I went upstairs to her room. Her room was turned upside down. Her mattress was cut open and her floor had a big hole in it.

"Khadijah, what happened, calm down come here?"

"Smoke left me."

"Why did he leave you, what happened?" Khadijah began to explain to me what happened. I couldn't believe Smoke or her. I'm not mad at Smoke that he took drastic measures to get her to stop selling dope. She knew better.

"Khadijah, calm down your still in the early stages of your pregnancy and I don't want you to lose your baby. I'm disappointed in you and Khadir.

I've done my job and I raised the two of you the best way I know how. Big KD is wrong for passing y'all his business. I don't want that for y'all at all. Do you see what the fuck I just went through? The FEDS was ready to hide my ass.

You have lost the love of your life behind this shit. Khadijah these streets don't love anybody out here. If someone really invaded your home. You would've been dead the moment they entered. It's up to you and what you're going to do the choice is yours. Go ahead and get dressed for your doctor's appointment. I'll go with you and where're your tools, so I can fix your door? I suggest that you move, who else knows what you were keeping here."

"I'm sorry Journee."

"Actions speak louder than words. I love you Khadijah go ahead and get dressed. I got you never question that." It's not funny but that's what the fuck Khadijah get. I fixed Khadijah's door and straightened her place up. Smoke and I sent a text back and forth I wish he would've recorded that shit.

Juelz

Journee has been gone all day. I had a special night planned for us. Jueleez was gone, she was with Nikki's for the night. It was just the two of us. Smoke told me what he did to Khadijah. I couldn't believe he still had it in him. Smoke was a real jack boy, he was known for kicking in doors and snatching keys.

I can only imagine what he did to Khadijah. I told Smoke he needs to take his ass home because Khadijah would want Journee to spend the night with her. I wasn't having that. I'm selfish as fuck It was a little after 8:00 pm. I heard the door open she must be home.

I had white and red roses filled throughout the room. The candles were lit. I filled the tub with a few rose petals. I heard Journee calling my name. I ignored her I had to finish my setup.

"Juelz." I continued to ignore her. Time hasn't been on my side lately. I wanted to do this days ago, but the opportunity didn't present itself. Today was the day no holding. I heard her walk up behind me.

"Juelz, all of this for me?"

"Who else, strip naked so I can take care of you." Journee did as she was told. I climbed into the tub right behind her. I placed my hands on her stomach she had a pudge. 8ball and MJG Space Age Pimping played blared through the speakers. A nigga ain't never done this shit before it was now or never.

"Journee, would you kill for me?"

"Yeah Juelz, if your life is in danger, never question that."

"I want you to prove it!"

"Would you steal for me?"

"Yeah, if that shit belongs to you."

"Will you marry me Journee?"

"Yes, if you're ready to jump the broom?" I pulled out the ring and slid it on her finger, she was amazed that smile was everything to me.

"Are you serious?"

"Will you marry me Journee? I want you to have my last name. I loved you the moment I laid eyes on you. It's nothing that I won't do for you and my children, but I refuse to let you bare another one of my children without giving you my last name."

"Yes, Juelz I will marry you." It was now or never. I loved Journee Leigh Armstrong with everything in me. She was it for me. We've been through it all together. It took a minute for us to get right, but here we are. I never gave up on her my soul wouldn't let me. I knew she was the one. I had to put in some work, but she was more than worth it.

Epilogue

Six months later

Khadir and Reagan are still going strong. Journee doesn't trust her for some reason. He's still heavy in the streets. Making major moves in Florida and Atlanta. Giselle and Dro are still seeing each other and taking it slow. Kassence adores him.

Khadijah and Smoke are trying to get along for the sake of their son. She's no longer selling dope anymore, she's back working a full-time job. Skeet and Nikki are still going strong she's expecting also, and she's having a boy.

Alexis and Alonzo are still kicking it heavy, their expecting a son also. Momma Edith, Pure, Majesty and Eboni came to the states to visit the girls. God Momma Valerie and Mrs. Simone the two of them are too much to handle.

Journee finally dissolved Kairo's estate. Momma Edith's overseeing the compounds in Ethiopia. Pure and Eboni are running the drug empire. Tyra's parents were killed. Journee and Juelz are expecting a boy also and planning a wedding. This is the end of Journee and Juelz, but you'll see some of the crew soon in a spin off coming to a Kindle near you soon.

THE END...

Check Out My Five Star Reads!!

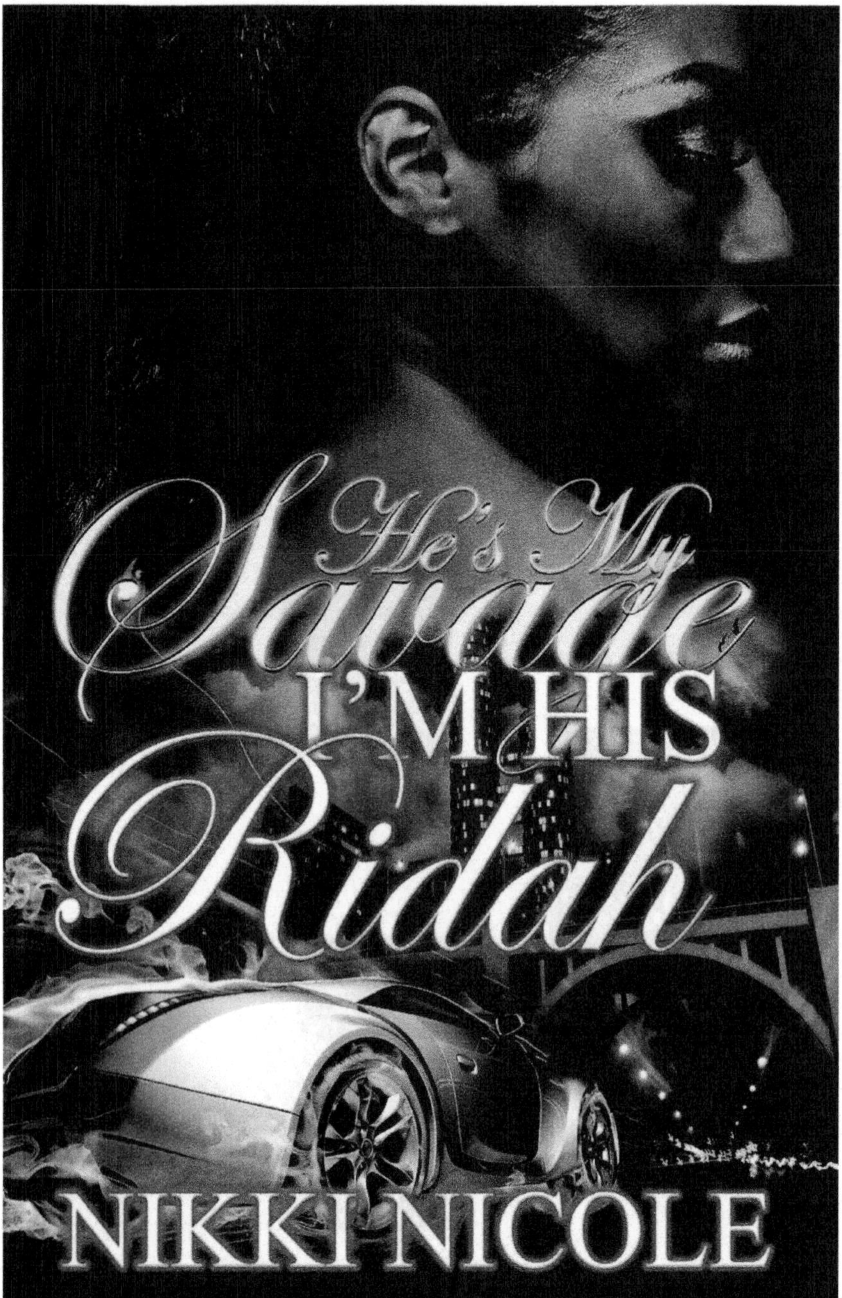
He's My
Savage
I'M HIS
Ridah
NIKKI NICOLE